POPULARITY HAS ITS UPS AND DOWNS

MEG F. SCHNEIDER

CONSULTING EDITOR DENNIS MEADE, Ph.D.

JULIAN MESSNER

Designed by Virginia Pope-Boehling

10 9 8 7 6 5 4 3 2 1

Library of Congress Cataloging-in-Publication Data

Schneider, Meg F.
    Popularity has its ups and downs/by Meg F. Schneider;
consulting editor, Dennis Meade.
        p. cm.
    Includes index.
    Summary: Explores the myths, limitations, and dangers of popularity and discusses how to develop true friendships and a confident sense of self-worth.
    1. Childhood friendship—Juvenile literature.   2. Popularity—Juvenile literature.   3. Self-confidence—Juvenile literature.   [1. Popularity.
2. Self-confidence.   3. Friendship.]   I. Meade, Dennis.   II. Title.
HQ784.F7S36 1992
158′.25—dc20   91-14477
                                                                                  CIP
                                                                                  AC
ISBN 0-671-72848-2   ISBN 0-671-72849-0 (pbk.)

CONTENTS

ONE

WHO WANTS TO BE POPULAR?

▲▼▲

hances are, since you've picked up this book, popularity is one of your concerns. This may be true for all kinds of reasons:

♦ You envy a popular girl or boy in school who seems to have endless fun.
♦ Your parents continually ask why you don't have more friends.
♦ You feel lonely a lot, as if you are always on the outside looking in.
♦ You're very popular right now, but you're terribly afraid it won't last.
♦ The kids in the most popular crowd in school ignore you.

Popularity can seem like the ultimate prize. After all, who wouldn't want to be liked and admired by lots of people? It's a powerful feeling to be showered with approval, looked upon with envy, and awarded a megadose of attention. Yes, popularity can be great. Except for one thing: you can't control it.

Popularity is a double-edged sword. It can make you feel wonderful, but it can also inspire fear. This is so for a good reason. Popularity does not belong to anyone. You can't give yourself popularity, and once you have it, you can't make it stay. Only *others* can give it, and *others* can take it away.

A person is popular because a group of people have chosen

him or her to admire, follow, and in some cases even imitate. This popular person may be generous and good or selfish and rather unkind. Frequently a person's character has little to do with why he or she is popular. What does count is that he or she may seem to have exciting qualities others wish were their own. Perhaps she is daring, exotic, or stylish. Perhaps he is competitive, rebellious, or successful with girls. We look upon these people with awe and make them popular. We do not necessarily like them, however.

A clear example of this can be seen in the way we admire a performer. Take Michael Jackson, for instance. He's extremely popular. People love his voice, his dancing, his white glove, and his unusual look. There's something about him that makes his fans feel good...that inspires them. These fans would say they adore him! But of course they don't. They adore his act. And they love the feeling of admiration they hold for him. It fills them with excitement and pleasure. Perhaps it's his daring to be different that fills them with joy. Maybe it's his videos that teeter on the brink of dangerous emotions. Whatever it is, Michael Jackson works hard for the attention he receives, and his fans continue to heap admiration upon him.

But that doesn't mean Michael Jackson's career is set for life. What happens when his fans see or hear someone else's act that fills them with even more awe?

And what happens to that popular person at school when someone new and more interesting enters the picture? His few true friends will probably stick by him, but what about everyone else?

It's fine that you would like to be popular. It can be great fun when you are in demand. But popularity is something you can never completely control. It does not come from you. It comes from other people who cannot give it to themselves either! It is a kind of favor that is bestowed on you.

That's why you should never confuse popularity and friendship—two words that are often used together but which have little to do with each other.

Yes, friendships, too, can fade away or even explode. But they are still, to a greater or lesser degree, within your control. Friendships are not given to you. They are something you and hopefully your friend work on. You can exercise tremendous influence over the way in which your friendships grow. Your sensitivity, honor, loyalty, intelligence, humor, and warmth all contribute to the path your friendships will follow.

But popularity does not necessarily depend on these traits. Of course if you treat everyone like garbage, you won't be popular. Still, there are plenty of people who, because of the way they act or look, attract a great deal of attention. It's not who they are as people that attracts the masses. It's who they seem to be. Which brings me to a very important question.

WHY ARE SOME PEOPLE POPULAR WHILE OTHERS ARE NOT?
▲▼▲

Some people are popular because of what we decide to see in them. Others are not popular because we cannot see the qualities we admire in them as easily. That doesn't mean they aren't there. It simply means those characteristics are not as readily apparent to us.

The truth is, people become popular mostly out of our need to aspire to something. We want to be more beautiful, more talented, more humorous, or more athletic, and so we find someone who appears to be all these things, and we grant that person power. What kind of power? The power to be what *we* want to be so that we can feel closer to our own dreams. What does this mean?

James was not terribly happy with his looks or his athletic abilities, but somehow he managed to get by because of his friendship with Mark, the best basketball player in junior high. It was fun to be with Mark. Kind of. Everyone gave James respect when he walked into the cafeteria with Mark or hung out with him at school dances. Girls even paid attention to James when he and Mark were together. Somehow when James was with Mark he felt like a much more exciting person.

Unfortunately, there is a danger to bestowing popularity upon someone. What if that popular person does not allow us to get near enough to feel as if we are becoming who we would most like to be?

Emily, a very cute eighth grader, never felt good-looking enough. But she was a member of the most popular group in her class and always felt particularly fine when she spent time with Tara, the girl everyone admired the most. Except, of course, when Tara ignored her, which she did on occasion. Tara traded confidences with a different person every week, and Emily felt like a big nothing when it wasn't her turn. She felt as if she were on a roller coaster. If Tara and she hung out together, Emily felt sure of herself and very pretty. If Tara spent time with another friend, Emily always found herself wondering what she'd done wrong and staring at herself in the mirror with something near to disgust.

It is a funny kind of irony that when we grant someone popularity in an effort to feel good about ourselves, we are putting ourselves down. Any time we put people up on pedestals, we remain below looking up at them. This is not a position of power. This is a position of weakness. Still, we continue to do so, hoping to find proof that we are as good as the people we admire. And what if you're the one on the pedestal? In some ways, it's a position of strength; in other ways, it's a vulnerable position. Imagine the fear of falling off! Which brings up the biggest problem of all.

YOU HAVE TO LIKE YOURSELF
▲▼▲

Any time we tie our self-esteem to how another person feels about us we are in very big trouble. No one can control the emotions and opinions of another person. You cannot make a person like you. You cannot make a person admire you. And most of all you cannot make another person responsible for making you feel good.

If you don't feel good about yourself, you will forever be a victim of popularity. If you are very popular, you will always worry about the day it might all disappear. If you are not very popular, you may spend all of your time trying to become more so. Either way, the voice of the crowd will occupy your emotional time, and you'll neglect your own interests, needs, and dreams.

So, is the point of all this that you should not want to be popular? Absolutely not! You should enjoy popularity. But you should also understand it so that you won't become dependent upon it.

Being popular can be great fun. It can make you feel important, keep you busy, and give you a special sense of belonging. If you're popular for some solid reasons, it can even introduce some wonderful friendships into your life.

But popularity, like everything else, is never exactly what it seems. It has its ups and downs. This usually comes as a great surprise to people, especially those who spend a lot of time feeling as if they are on the outside looking in. They imagine that popularity is an endless party.

Well, it isn't.

Remember that people are popular because of what we choose to see in them. But what we see in them is not always really there! As we will see later on in this book, we often imagine that this popular person has qualities that may in fact not exist.

So not only is popularity not all it seems to be, but very often neither is the popular person!

When it comes to popularity, there's a lot more going on than usually meets the eye.

PUTTING POPULARITY IN ITS PLACE
▲▼▲

Popularity as an issue will never completely go away. No matter how old you are, the desire to be admired and liked will stay with you. But you can feel popular no matter how many people surround you. You may have no control over the trappings of popularity—how many people call you or imitate you or want to be near you—but you can still enjoy many of the feelings you imagine popularity will bring. You can do so by knowing and liking yourself, by building a network of solid friendships, and by gaining a new understanding about what popularity really means.

You can feel well liked. You can feel admired. And you can feel sought-after. But before that can happen you have to learn to appreciate your own value. In fact, you should start working on that immediately, which is why you will find a section called "Confidence Builders" at the end of each chapter. These are easy, enlightening exercises designed to help you put an end to those old "I'm not good enough" feelings. Each group of exercises will relate to the message of the specific chapter so that you will be able to use your new insights to help you work toward a more positive view of yourself.

Popularity can be fleeting. You deserve more than that. When people say they want to be popular, what they really mean is they want to have good friends and feel good about themselves.

That's absolutely in your control. And that is what this book is about. Once you put popularity in its place and make room in your life for the real you, life will be a lot easier!

TWO

THE GREAT POPULARITY MYTHS

—————— ▲▼▲ ——————

People imagine that popularity promises fabulous things. Sometimes they strive toward it as if everything else has no importance. Unfortunately, this can create a number of problems. If you have held popularity up as a precious goal, you need to consider the price you may be paying for such a small reward.

Overestimating the value of popularity could leave you striving for something that doesn't really exist. While you are wasting your time pursuing popularity, people who do care for the real you could be falling by the wayside. Then, if one day you are finally labeled "popular"—whatever you think that means—you are bound to feel very disappointed and awfully confused. It is not the glorious cure-all for life's problems. You may still find yourself with concerns and hurts that need attention. Also by mythologizing popularity you may not be giving popular people a fair shake, or giving yourself a real break. By failing to see popular people as they really are, you cheat them out of being truly understood and accepted. By idealizing them, you can fail to see your own self-worth. Remember? The higher the pedestal, the farther down you tend to be!

7

For weeks, Penny had been trying to befriend Janette, one of the most popular girls in her class. She let Janette copy her math notes, agreed with almost everything she said, and complimented her every day. Finally, Janette appeared to be warming to her, and Penny's spirits began to soar. At last she was being accepted into the most popular crowd at school, where everyone looked good and had tons of friends. It was unimaginable to Penny that Janette and her buddies could ever be unhappy. That was why Penny could not believe it when she found Janette crying her eyes out in the girls' room because someone had criticized her hair.

If you're going to aspire to popularity—and there's nothing wrong with wanting to be admired, have lots of friends, and feel confident—you need to understand the truth about popularity. That way if you get there you won't be bitterly disappointed or unprepared, and if you don't become popular, you won't spend all your time wishing you had. Seeing popularity for what it really is, stripped of all the mythology, will help you put it into a perspective. It will still look attractive, but it won't glitter like gold.

Here's a look at the most common myths about popularity and why you shouldn't believe them.

MYTH #1: POPULAR PEOPLE ARE WELL LIKED

Being popular does not necessarily mean being well liked. If a popular person also happens to be thoughtful and great fun, he or she might indeed be well liked. But popularity does not guarantee the genuine affection of others.

Sometimes people become popular because they look great, do daring things, or seem sophisticated. But none of these traits has to do with who they are as people. They are admired for their image, the picture they present. People are attracted to this image because it seems to promise so much!

The athletic person may seem powerful and exciting, and the sophisticated person, interesting and mysterious. As a consequence, they may be surrounded by people who compliment them profusely, imitate them in every way, and fashion every remark they make in accordance with what they think this popular person wants to hear.

But this is not affection. This is a form of idolatry—not to mention deceit! Here we go again with that pedestal. If you idolize someone, you make that person better than you. If you say things just to please him or her, you are being dishonest. Without equality and truthfulness, there can be no real friendship between you and that popular person.

Of course, popular people who are well liked sometimes lose their popularity, but they won't lose their friends. The crowd may grow tired of this person's antics, or that person's daring, or another's appearance. But the people who like them for who they are will continue to do so. Warmth, good humor, generosity, and other positive traits don't ever go out of style.

MYTH #2: POPULAR PEOPLE ARE HAPPY

Popular people who are also well liked are probably quite happy. They are admired by lots of people, and they have good friends to boot. But they also have concerns. Sometimes very popular people have a lot of responsibilities and too much attention. Since so many people are looking at them, the pressure to do the right thing, or to "perform," can be tremendous. Sometimes it's easier to accomplish things when no one is watching and waiting.

Of course, popular people who are not really well liked but are merely "in" feel themselves on shaky ground. They fear losing all of the attention. Usually, in their hearts, they know the difference between being truly liked and being admired or envied. Often these people feel they have to work very hard to hold on to their popularity. And they do work hard. They are, after all, often putting on a performance. If they let it lapse they could lose the crowd. This is a very unhappy way to move through life. It's so much easier and far more pleasant simply to be yourself. It's sad to feel that your friendships depend on how funny you are or how fast you run instead of on who you are.

Peter's tennis match was about to start, but he couldn't get himself to leave the locker room. He felt everyone was counting on him. His friends were even planning a party for him after the match. That made Peter feel sick. It wasn't that he thought he'd lose his reputation as Lake Junior High's number one player. He just didn't want to look at his friends' faces if he lost. All anyone seemed to want to talk about was his next match. Sometimes he wished he could be the one no one expected to win. But that was impossible. So he sat in the locker room, tense and unhappy, fervently wishing he were on an Amazon riverboat.

MYTH #3: POPULAR PEOPLE ARE SUPER CONFIDENT

It is not true that popularity brings confidence. Everyone harbors insecurities. Some people just hide them better than others. Even the most popular teenagers occasionally think that others do not consider them athletic, smart, good-looking, or fun. It may appear to you that someone has it all. But few people ever feel that way about themselves. And for good reason—no one ever *does* have it all.

Unfortunately, popular people often feel forced to act confident. They feel it is a part of their image that they must uphold at all costs. Sometimes this is easy. On certain days they may feel absolutely wonderful. But on other days they may not. Faking confidence can be exhausting, depressing, and off-putting.

Popular people are in a bind. They feel they need to act confident because that's what others expect. As a consequence, they often don't reach for the emotional support and encouragement they need. This ends up distancing people, making others feel that they simply can't relate to those who always act so sure of themselves. What a shame. It would help popular people to feel they can show some weaknesses. And it would help the not-so-popular to see that everyone has moments of insecurity.

MYTH #4: POPULAR PEOPLE ONLY WANT TO HANG OUT WITH THE "IN" CROWD

Sometimes popular people don't befriend kids from other crowds. One reason for this is that those "other crowds" don't seem interested in offering their friendship. Probably the less popular kids are afraid to extend an invitation and risk being rejected. Another reason is that popular people are often made to feel as if they are betraying their own crowd by stepping outside of their private circle. They might even be accused of "getting weird" or "changing"—accusations that can make them afraid of losing their position. In other words, popular people are often isolated from those with whom they might enjoy a terrific relationship. The truth is, they often wish they could move outside their own crowd and find new friends.

René was great looking and very sophisticated. All the girls flocked around her, eager to be her buddy. None of them realized how lonely René sometimes felt, largely because René never dared talk about that. She kept her sadness and her unhappy family life to herself. At midyear, however, a new girl named Meg entered the class, and René immediately liked her. She was different, but she seemed very smart and quite talented. René admired her. Since Meg was new, a lot of girls gave her a hard time, but René befriended her—until two of her "friends" started saying things like "How can you be friends with us and with her, too?" Reluctantly, René started pulling away from Meg. She also went back to keeping many secrets about herself.

MYTH #5: POPULAR PEOPLE MAKE OTHERS FEEL SMALL

Only you can make yourself feel small. Feeling inferior when you're with a popular person has more to do with your opinion of yourself than with anything that popular person is doing. The truth is, the unkind thoughts others have about us will sting only if they match our own thoughts and fears about ourselves. Think about it. You're standing with two girls discussing the number of times they were asked to dance at a Saturday night party. You grow angrily silent because you were not asked as often as they were. You think to yourself, "I hate them. They are making me feel terrible." Well, the truth is, *you* are making yourself feel terrible. These two girls may be a little insensitive, but they are not responsible for your feelings about yourself. If you listened to them and said to yourself, "I wouldn't have wanted to dance with half the guys who asked them anyway," you might actually find it funny.

If you are able to stay aware of your own special and unique qualities, you will feel just fine in the presence of a popular person.

MYTH #6: POPULAR PEOPLE THINK THEY'RE BETTER THAN OTHERS

Well-liked people have too much respect for the strengths and importance of the people around them to feel better than all of them. Sure, they probably think they are better looking than some, and perhaps more athletic, intelligent, or talented than a few others. And maybe they are. Jim, a very popular ninth grader, may in fact be a better ballplayer than

Sam. On the other hand, Sam might have a sense of humor that makes everyone laugh—a trait Jim deeply envies. Jim doesn't feel better than Sam. He's pleased with his own strengths and, like everyone else, wishes he had more.

As for the less well-liked popular people—surprise!—they probably spend much of their time feeling that they aren't as good as many of the people who admire them! People who spend most of their time creating an image are sometimes the most insecure. They may feel that they are simply not interesting enough to get the love and attention they crave, and so they create an exciting role for themselves, and they play it for all it's worth. Underneath they are terribly afraid someone will realize they are not as interesting as they seem.

These people are doing themselves a terrible injustice, because they *are* special. Everyone is. But what's special is the stuff that comes naturally, not the role they play.

MYTH #7: POPULAR PEOPLE HAVE MANY FRIENDS

That very much depends on how you define "friends." If you mean they always have someone around with whom to make plans, maybe you're right. But the assumption that they are never lonely and that there is always someone around in whom they can confide is misguided.

The truth is that popular people probably have the same number of good friends as anyone else. Popular or not, everyone has a distinctive personality and distinctive desires. Friendships are special matches in which both people can give and receive exactly what they need. This kind of relationship is not easy to come by. It takes trust. It takes openness, and it means finding the right people with whom one can share this special bond. In short, friendship requires work, and it is no easier for popular people than it is for anyone else.

Popular people can absolutely be lonely! Just because there are a lot of people floating around them does not mean they can confide in any of them. Have you ever heard of "being lonely in a crowd"? Sometimes being around lots of people actually stands in the way of reaching out and finding that all-important connection with another person.

Popular people don't have more friends than anyone else. They are just a little busier!

Popularity, as you can see, is not the answer to whatever ill feeling you may harbor about yourself or the world around you. It can't take away the supposed flaws you perceive within yourself. It can't change the problems you might have at home or at school. And it cannot make you feel good about yourself. That has to come from inside you. Yes, the way you feel about yourself is colored by how others react to you. If you treat people kindly and they respond warmly, that will make you feel good about yourself. But in the end it's your own sense of your own self-worth that matters the most.

Besides, the better you feel about yourself, the better others will feel about you. It's the person who has confidence from within who attracts the most solid friendships.

CONFIDENCE BUILDERS
▲▼▲

Just as we tend to mythologize popular people by imagining that they are bigger than life, so do we often make the mistake of mythologizing our own flaws by thinking they are more terrible than they really are. It isn't easy to look at ourselves realistically. Somehow our anxieties and insecurities always get in the way. But here are some exercises to help you shrink those "giant" flaws of yours back to size!

CRITICIZE THE PART, NOT THE WHOLE

When you do something wrong, don't criticize the whole you. In other words, if you say something silly, don't think, "Boy, am I dumb." Instead, say to yourself, "That was a dumb thing to say." Keep the blunder in perspective. Think back to the times when you were proud of the remarks you made and the thoughts you expressed. Remember that everyone says dumb things sometimes. As soon as you stop attacking yourself on a broad basis, you will stop blowing your flaws up out of proportion. That way you can still like yourself even if you don't like something you did.

- If you do poorly on a math test, don't think, "I'm stupid." Instead, think, "I'll study harder next time. Too bad I'm not as good in math as I am in history."
- If you don't tell jokes well, don't think, "I'm not funny." Instead, remind yourself that you sometimes say humorous things when you're not trying.

CHASE THOSE BLACK THOUGHTS AWAY

All of us entertain negative thoughts about ourselves. None of us feels good about his or herself all of the time. If you lack self-confidence, chances are you beat yourself up with a lot of negative thoughts that have no basis in reality. You may even be standing in the way of finding some solutions that could help you feel a lot better. It is a good idea, therefore, to get into the practice of "arguing" with your worst thoughts. Countering your worst feeling with positive facts will help to bring things into perspective:

No one likes me	Mike and Pete have been my friends for a long time. Sure it would be nice to be liked by everyone, but who is? How many friends does anyone need? I think I'll invite Mike and Pete over to watch a movie with me.
I am ugly	I don't like my nose, but my figure is nice, and Patti says with a little makeup my eyes would look gorgeous.

| I'm the only one who gets lonely | I took a walk around the school grounds yesterday afternoon. There were a lot of people sitting alone who looked a little sad. |
| I'm not athletic | I don't play tennis well, but I'm a fast runner. I should try out for the track team. Runners are athletes, too. |

THREE

WHO IS THE
REAL YOU?

—————————— ▲▼▲ ——————————

One of the toughest jobs we face on our way to becoming a confident, well-adjusted, and happy person is figuring out who we really are. It's a job we must undertake again and again as we pass through new stages in our lives.

It would seem at first glance that doing so would be a snap. After all, you live with yourself. Who should know better than you how you feel about things.

Well, it's true that you live with yourself. But you are a very complicated person filled with all kinds of insecurities, strengths, fears, and dreams. You cannot always see yourself clearly.

Also, you don't live alone. Everyday in every way you are subjected to the opinions, thoughts, confusion, compliments, insults, criticism, applause, approval, disapproval, and prejudices of others. No matter what your impression of yourself, your needs, your accomplishments, or your desires, there is always someone out there who disagrees, who challenges the way you see things.

As you get older the challenges of others will affect you less. You will have had many experiences that confirm your view of yourself, and so the disapproval of others will not be so confusing. (It's always a little hurtful!) But when you're younger and struggling to maintain a sense of who you are and what you need, feel, and believe, the ground can feel very shaky. In fact, your opinions about yourself may change in accordance with the last person you speak to.

Keith had just finished playing his favorite Mozart sonata at a piano recital. He felt wonderful. He'd played it with feeling and gusto, and except for a minor mistake in the second movement, he'd hardly missed a note. The applause felt wonderful. Proudly he took his seat next to a fellow performer, who smiled at him sympathetically and said, "You must have been nervous." Keith's shoulders slumped, and he spent the rest of the recital obsessing about who else had heard the "massive error" he had made.

It is important for you to have as clear a sense of yourself as possible. Don't be tempted to mold yourself into the kind of person others want you to be. This will only lead to disaster, because we can only be who we are. We can pretend otherwise for a time, but doing so will inevitably lead to unhappiness and loneliness.

Let's start to explore who you truly are and to evaluate the major influences on you. I say "start," because that's as far as we can go. You are probably changing every day, as are many of the people in your life. Still, here is your chance to carefully consider all of the important things about you, both positive and negative, that deserve respect and make you unique. And here is an opportunity for you to see the criticisms of others in a new light—and to recognize that your sense of who you are is the most important thing of all.

Getting to know and appreciate yourself is the first step toward enjoying true friendships and feeling popular in your own special way.

GETTING THE FACTS
▲▼▲

Who are you? To get a full picture of that complicated creature who is you, we have to take a look at the separate aspects of yourself. These are your (1) personality traits, (2) your talents or strengths, (3) your weaknesses, (4) your beliefs, (5) your actions and activities, (6) your likes and dislikes, and (7) your looks.

As you do these exercises, try to be objective. Consider what you believe to be true about yourself in combination with observations other people have made of you that you feel may be true. Write down whatever comes to mind, even if some contradictions appear. A person can be both bad-tempered and sweet, for example.

Remember, this is just a starting point for you to discover more about the real you.

YOUR PERSONALITY TRAITS

Your personality traits are reflected in the way you behave and feel. Take a moment to review how you react in different circumstances—from the lunchroom to the classroom, from the baseball game to your home. Write down the character traits you believe amount to the real you. Here are some examples:

Impatient	Honest	Tense	Stubborn
Shy	Relaxed	Short-tempered	Aggressive
Angry	Distant	Generous	Unassertive
Loving	Sensitive	Upbeat	Head-strong
Understanding	Tentative	Indirect	Flexible
Gentle	Secretive	Bitter	Talkative
Open			

Most people have contradictory traits. They may be very

impatient sometimes and extremely patient at other times. They may be hot-tempered in some circumstances and endlessly calm in others. This is because when we speak of personality traits, we are talking about your capacity or tendency to behave in a certain way, not how you act at every moment. If you write down opposites don't be confused. In different circumstances and in different moods you may respond in different ways. Of course this will make you a little difficult to label, but that's just as well. Applying labels to yourself is useless. They will always be wrong because no one is ever just one way.

YOUR TALENTS OR STRENGTHS

What are the things you feel most comfortable doing, the things you enjoy and have the most success pursuing? You don't have to be world-class! Just write down those areas in which you feel the strongest. Here are some examples of talents and abilities:

Playing the piano	Drawing	Running	Solving math
Making friends	Swimming	track	problems
Debating	Writing	Babysitting	Writing
Telling jokes	Dancing	Designing	poetry
Cheering others up	Knitting	outfits	

Talent has to do with the particular abilities with which we are born, but it also has to do with our self-image, the expectations of others, our interests, and our drive. Unfortunately people have a tendency to take for granted what they do well—unless it's something that is very "in" at the moment—and instead find fault with themselves for the things at which they are not good. If you are not an agile dancer, you may feel that having the grace of a swan would be the most wonderful gift. But, chances are, if you suddenly displayed a gift for dance, there'd be something else you couldn't do that seemed even more important. So give yourself a break. Think about how great some of the things you can do really are. Get in touch with the pride you are entitled to.

YOUR WEAKNESSES

No one is good at everything. We all have weaknesses. Still, as we discussed earlier, it's easy to blow a weakness way out of proportion.

Being as specific as possible, given what you learned in the last chapter under "Confidence Builders," write down the particular weaknesses you believe are your own. Don't generalize. It's very important to pinpoint the thing you find disappointing because doing so will keep you from viewing the weakness as more widespread than it actually is. For example:

♦ I can't fast dance (instead of, I can't dance).
♦ I can't spell (instead of, I'm terrible in English).
♦ I talk a lot when I'm nervous (instead of, I talk too much).

It is important to recognize your weaknesses, to say to yourself "I am not that good at..." or "Unfortunately, I have a tendency to..." Facing a sense of disappointment in yourself is a very powerful move. It means you are not afraid to face your imperfections. It also means you have no intention of wasting time hiding from them or allowing them to color all the positive things you do feel about yourself. If you are willing to look at your weaknesses and say, "I'm not afraid to see you," then they won't have a chance of secretly and silently wearing away at your self-image.

YOUR BELIEFS

All of us have a belief system that governs the way we see the world and treat others. What are the things you hold to be true that have a great deal to do with why you think and behave the way you do? Don't stop with your immediate surroundings. Consider your political and religious beliefs as well. Here are some examples of beliefs:

+ I think it's cruel to tease people.
+ I don't think ethnic jokes and comments are funny.
+ I think all students should have a chance to be on a team, even if they don't play well.
+ I am committed to my religion.
+ I think more money should be spent on homeless people and less on defense.

It is important to keep in mind that beliefs can change. As we move through life and have more experiences, we will come to see things in new ways. What we once thought was true, we may come to believe is no longer so. It is critical that you give yourself room to change your mind, to be open to new beliefs. Clinging to a belief simply because it feels safe and familiar will only lead you right back to wondering who you are.

YOUR ACTIONS AND ACTIVITIES

How do you spend your days? Begin with the most obvious routine activities. Here is your chance to take an objective look at the different activities you juggle in a day. Let's start with some examples of actions or activities:

+ Riding the bus
+ Grocery shopping on Saturday mornings
+ Baby-sitting on Tuesday nights
+ Homework every afternoon except Friday
+ Drying dinner dishes
+ Pizza on Fridays with Gina
+ Tennis lessons on Wednesday afternoons

You accomplish a lot in a given day. That's something of which to be proud. Still, at the end of a day you might glumly sit around thinking, "I didn't get anything done today."

That's probably untrue. Attending school, participating in soccer practice, and being home in time for dinner is plenty. But even that's not the point.

In the course of a given day we might take a lot of subtle actions that are extremely important, but which we tend to ignore. Cheering up a friend, for example. And what about the fifteen minutes or so you spend rinsing out cans and plastics for recycling? You may not think the way you spend your day says anything about you. So much of it, like going to school, seems as if it has already been planned for you. But it's important to give yourself credit for all the things you do for yourself and for others during an ordinary day.

Take a moment now and add those less obvious accomplishments to your list. Did you help a friend with a science experiment? Find a missing toy for your younger brother? Bring your tired father the newspaper?

Cheering up a friend or making an effort to protect the planet says something good about who you are. Take a long look at the list you drew up and consider the energy it took to do everything. Think about the sense of responsibility you must have and the way people rely on you. All of these qualities and more are reflected in the way you spend your day.

YOUR LIKES AND DISLIKES

Almost everyone has strong likes and dislikes. Who knows why? The reasons are many and often don't matter. What are yours? List anything that comes to mind. Here are some examples:

I like:

◆ Hiking
◆ Playing cards
◆ Painting
◆ Going to baseball games
◆ Eating chocolate ice cream

I dislike:

♦ Bowling
♦ Track
♦ Cleaning out the garage
♦ Shopping
♦ Eating chili
♦ Sleeping bags

We are all entitled to our different likes and dislikes. They are a reflection of the unique aspects of our personality that make each of us so different from the next. Unfortunately, some people, in order to be popular or to feel as if they belong, will pretend to have the same likes and dislikes as "the crowd." It's as if they feel they can only be friends if they think alike. But in truth, the best kinds of friends are the ones who respect each other's differences. That's how people learn and grow. So admit to what you like and don't like and make sure you are sensitive to the feelings of others. Your true friends will allow for your preferences if you allow for theirs.

YOUR LOOKS

This is a very sensitive subject. It's very hard to be objective about one's looks. Usually we are too critical about the way we appear. Take a step back, and without making judgments describe yourself as accurately as you can. For example you might list:

Blue almond-shaped eyes
Straight shoulder length hair
Small waist
Long arms
Wide nose

The only reason that looks are included on the list of elements that compose the real you is because of how they make you feel. Looks are very deceiving. They actually reveal very little about who you really are. Big blue eyes say nothing about a person. An athletic build doesn't even mean a person is a good athlete! The truth is your body language says more about who you are than any particular feature of your face or body.

Unfortunately, especially when you are younger, people place a tremendous amount of importance on their looks. It's as if they define themselves by their appearance. If they look good they must be great. If they don't look so attractive they must be pretty worthless. Fortunately as we get older we wise up! Perhaps this is because as we develop our talents, abilities, and interests we begin to see ourselves in more "whole" ways. The very fact that we feel proud of an accomplishment makes who we see in the mirror more attractive.

Perhaps one of the most cruel things that young people do to themselves is to obsess about their physical imperfections. So much so that they forget to enhance the positive.

Ali, a very pretty redhead with beautiful green eyes, took one look in the department store mirror and wanted to cry. One bathing suit looked worse than another and the weekend was only three days away. "If only my legs were a little longer," she muttered to herself with despair as she quickly took off the suit... forgetting altogether to try on the matching sarong skirt that would have given her a considerably elongated look.

Few of us will ever look like the stars on movie and TV screens. And the truth is, few of them look as great in the flesh as they do on celluloid! Very few people look in the mirror in the morning and like everything they see. The trouble is that when we are feeling low it's easy to center on our flaws... and to block out all other delightful characteristics. But as with everything else you have to look at the whole! Every piece! Not just that one small problem. Because small problems become very big ones when they are the only things you are thinking about.

You've now had the chance to consider the facts. Some of these facts may feel a bit unimportant, confusing, or contradictory to you. But often these are the parts of you that are the most interesting! In fact, the smallest details and contradictions inside of you are the things that make you special. Of course it's not just the contradictions within that make it difficult for people to stay in touch with who they really are. It's also the people around them.

You do not live alone. There are probably a lot of people in your life who let you know what they think of you. Sometimes what they say will feel good and other times it will hurt. When it's very painful you might even start to feel that maybe they are correct and that you are not as good as you thought....

So, in an effort to help you understand why people may offer criticisms that you think are unjust, and to keep you from all too quickly concluding, "Well, I guess I'm not so great..." read on...

WHAT OTHERS SAY ABOUT YOU

Throughout your life people will be forming opinions of you. Their opinions will be quite important to you because many times it is the conclusions they draw that will determine some of the things that happen to you. Was your book report good? Do you listen well in class? Should you be allowed to graduate? Are you responsible enough to babysit or mow the lawn for a neighbor? Are you mature enough to go on a camping trip by yourself?

But there is one opinion about you that counts more than any other. And that is *yours*.

Certainly it is very important to consider the criticisms

and compliments that are sent in your direction. It is very difficult to be objective about oneself and we all need improving. But always, you should keep in mind that the opinions of others are colored by two things. The way we choose to act with this person, and that person's own particular way of seeing things, which is colored by his or her own problems or issues.

Many people in your life have probably formed opinions about who you are. Teachers, parents, friends, and neighbors have all had opportunities to observe you and interact with you. From these experiences they have drawn a number of conclusions about you.

But it's a funny thing about those conclusions. They may all be quite different from one another and may even be contradictory. A teacher may feel you're lazy. But a neighbor whose fence you painted might think you industrious. Your sister may feel you are thoughtless and selfish, but your good friend might believe you to be attentive and caring.

And do you know why this is?

Because they are all right, to some degree.

This happens because you display different qualities at different moments. When people are annoyed or dismayed with your behavior, they will criticize that momentary you. They forget to consider the whole you. Certainly we hope people will look past our occasional blunders and see that we are not always mean or selfish or slow or annoying. We hope they will say, "Today you behaved selfishly, but basically you are a wonderful friend." But sometimes they don't. (Do you?)

This brings us to the next important point: people see us in their own personal way. Everyone has problems. Everyone experiences things in accordance with the good or bad feelings they bring along with them. After you receive three C-minuses in a row, a teacher who is overworked might conclude that you need to be put into the slower math class. In fact, all you need is an hour or so of tutorial help to clarify a concept with which you are having difficulty. A parent who has had a terrible day at work and who accuses you of being irresponsible when you forget to do an errand may be reacting more to his or her own problems than to your weaknesses.

Philip arrived home on Saturday after a heated game of soccer to find his father waiting impatiently for him in the kitchen. "I thought you and I were going to clean out the garage this morning," he snapped. "You are incredibly irresponsible." Philip, who adored his father, looked away, shaken. He retreated to his room, put his head in his hands, and sighed heavily. "It's true," he thought. "I am irresponsible." But Philip forgot two things. Just the other day, all by himself, he'd rushed his little sister to the emergency room after she fell off her bike. His parents had praised him for taking charge of the situation. He also forgot that yesterday his father found out his company had been sold and that his job was no longer secure.

Listen to what others say about you. Very often they will be right, in a way. You may be lazy in some circumstances and not others. You may not be a stellar math student, but maybe you can turn that around. If you have behaved irresponsibly, own up to that fact. But don't torture yourself with the notion that you are a totally irresponsible person. It may not be true! There have probably been lots of times when you behaved responsibly.

Ultimately you have to believe in yourself. If you can do that, popularity will seem far less important. You will have become popular with yourself.

And what does that mean?

It means you will enjoy being you. You will feel that you are worth being admired, imitated, and liked. Best of all, it will matter very little whether lots of people agree with that conclusion. If you have a few good friends and one of them is you, that is more than enough!

CONFIDENCE BUILDERS
▲▼▲

Knowing who you are is important, but so is having faith in who you are. Believing in yourself will help you face the criticism of others. It will give you the strength to accept what is true and reject what is not. And having faith in yourself has another benefit. It will give you the confidence you need to keep striving, to improve, and to take on new challenges.

STAND UP FOR THE WHOLE YOU

If you do something wrong or hurtful and someone accuses you of being a terrible person, don't accept the criticism. Admit to your mistakes, but do not allow your entire self to be called into question. "You're right. I didn't think about your feelings last night at all. I'm sorry. But I have helped you a lot in the past. I am not a bad person." And if people criticize you unjustly, say so. Don't immediately start to doubt yourself. Listen to what others have to say, and if you think they're wrong, say so and explain why. "I did not lie to you. I told you I was busy that night and I was. You didn't ask me what I was doing, and I honestly didn't think it mattered."

DEVELOP A SPECIAL SKILL

Concentrate on learning a skill, developing a talent, or mastering a particular area of interest. Becoming a specialist in one subject or being particularly good at something can be a real confidence builder. Others will admire your special abilities. You will feel their approval, and you'll be encouraged to be even better. And in the process, you will be building a sense of real self-worth. It will start with being able to say, "I know a lot about stamp collecting." After a while that positive feeling will spill out into other areas, and pretty soon you will be saying to yourself, "I really am worth something."

FOUR

YOU AND MR. OR MS. POPULAR

▲▼▲

Now that you have come to know a bit more about the real you, it's time to consider what the real you needs. More specifically, you are now better able to determine what you need in a friendship and with whom you are most likely to get it. Needs are those things you require from people to fulfill you, satisfy you, and bring you happiness.

Popular kids can be fun to hang around. But they are no better or worse friends than anyone else. Good friendships spring up between people whose personalities are a good match. Popularity cannot make a person a good friend because it isn't a personality trait. But popularity can make you *think* that a person might be a fabulous friend! And that is where trouble often begins.

Sometimes when we intensely admire or envy someone we forget to think about why. We're so preoccupied with our own feelings and so busy yearning to be like that person that we stop seeing who he or she really is. In our struggle to win over Mr. or Ms. Popular, we forget to determine if we even like this person. The need to bask in his or her glory is too intense.

What a terrible waste of time! Why crave a friendship

31

with Mr. and Ms. Popular when, deep down, you care very little about who they really are? What a deceitful thing to do! At this point you might well be feeling a bit indignant. "What do you mean I don't like her?" you might say. "She is the most popular kid in the class! She's so funny! And she's just beginning to like me!" Well, already you've seen that this "most popular" girl may not actually be the way you perceive her to be.

Now let's introduce another possibility. Maybe this whole popular crowd is not made up of people with whom you feel really comfortable. Forget about whether or not they wish to include you. Maybe you are a person who has needs they could never fulfill.

In this chapter we are going to explore the possibility that you do not know or perhaps even like that group of kids you have labeled "popular." The goal is to help you start fresh, to point you in the direction of people who can fulfill your needs. Maybe you could enjoy a sincere friendship with *some* "popular" kids. But if that's true, it's because of who they really are and who you really are—not because everyone else wants to be near them.

Jyl at long last found herself a member of the most popular crowd in school. She had dropped a lot of weight the summer before. And her new haircut and stylish new clothes made her feel great. She still remained somewhat friendly with her old pals, but she threw herself into the popular Alissa's social circle with a great deal of pleasure. It was great fun at first. Alissa and her two closest friends knew lots of guys, and pretty soon Jyl was sharing confidences with them. But then Jyl began to feel uncomfortable. Alissa, she noticed, was lots of fun and full of energy, but she wasn't particularly loyal. She put down her two closest friends a lot, and Jyl wasn't used to that. She never criticized Martha, her old good friend, with anyone, even if she was mad at her. One day while Alissa was telling Jyl a particularly unflattering story about her two buddies, Jyl was struck by a terrible thought: "I wonder what she says about me behind my back."

Often when we finally get what we think we want most in life, it is not at all what we had expected. If we had paused in our pursuit to give it a long, hard look we might have been able to see this in advance. But most times we don't.

Well, here's your chance to end the chase. Here's your opportunity to take a closer look at what you crave. The goal is not to stop wanting it. You may still seek to be close to a certain popular person. And that's fine, as long as it's for the right reasons.

You need to know exactly what you are going after so that when and if you get it you won't have wasted your time. You will have known what to expect, and you should feel good about what you have attained.

Popular kids make great friends... as long as you really like them!

ARE YOU A GOOD MATCH?
▲▼▲

What are the traits you feel you need in a friend? List them on a separate piece of paper. Be sure to note the qualities your friends now offer you as well as the ones they appear to lack. Let your mind wander. Naturally you won't be able to find all of the qualities you list in any one person, but don't let that stop you. Get in touch with the traits you crave in your ideal friend. Here are some examples:

Loyal	Honest
Warm	Sensitive
Funny	Adventurous
Politically committed	Tactful
Good listener	Cheerful
Straightforward	Serious

It's important to know what you need in a friendship. It's also critical to establish how you expect to be treated. That way when you are faced with the unpleasant reality of someone letting you down or treating you poorly you won't become confused. You won't think it's your fault for being too demanding. And if you have a popular friend with whom things are not working, you will see that it is a poor match instead of blaming everything on your inadequacy.

Consider the person you most admire, the one (or two) with whom you imagine a friendship would be fabulous. On the list you have just made circle the traits you are quite sure this admired or popular person can claim. Don't confuse what you assume is true with what you know to be so. Circle only what you know as fact. This doesn't mean he or she isn't sensitive or honest. But if you haven't seen any evidence of this trait, don't circle it.

If a very popular person proves not to be such a great friend, you tend to feel horribly surprised and disappointed. You may even blame the struggle on yourself. Of course, all of your friends will let you down at one time or another, and it's important at such times to talk the problem through and forgive them. But if you are blinded by someone's popularity you may neglect to see that you and this person are not a good match. He or she is not capable of meeting your particular needs. Except for one, of course—your need to be near a popular person.

List all the things you don't particularly like about the popular crowd or person. Even if it seems small—for example, you don't really like the jokes one boy tells—place it on your list. Now consider the reasons behind your dislike. If you don't like his jokes, why not? Are they racist, or do they make fun of other kids? What could this mean about this person?

Once we decide that someone is worth liking the tendency is to make lots of excuses for anything the person might do that troubles us. This is only fair. The truth is, there will always be things about a friend that we wish were different. The trouble begins, however, when that something is quite important and we still tell ourselves that it doesn't matter. Keeping an honest open mind is critical. For one thing, it allows us to see when we are pursuing something that may, in fact, be all wrong for us. And, for another, it may leave us open to liking people in whom we formerly had no interest.

Now list the things you like most about this very popular person or crowd. Write down anything that comes to mind. Consider what people look like, think about, are interested in, and laugh about. Examine any aspect of their personalities that has to do with your attraction to them. For example:

♦ He makes me laugh.
♦ She thinks for herself.
♦ He dresses with unbelievable style.
♦ She can talk with anyone about anything.
♦ He's a great athlete.

How well do you know this popular person? You might be so anxious to befriend popular people for superficial reasons that you don't stop to get to know them. Of course, this does neither one of you justice. You may be hanging out with someone who is all wrong for you, or perhaps this person has a lot to give, but you aren't even noticing because you like the way he or she dresses. It's important to get to know someone before you decide beyond a shadow of a doubt the friendship is something you need to have. If your list seems silly, maybe you should dig a little deeper.

When you are with this person, how do you feel? Think of a particular situation in which you were both involved. Write down the emotions below and add a few that you can remember feeling during and after the encounter:

Excited	Proud	Happy
Offended	Tired	Angry
Horrible	Unimpressed	Sad
Confused	Nervous	Bored
Upset	Relaxed	Interested

Sometimes when we finally get what we've wanted, we

are so excited that we don't think about whether or not we're happy! The only way to be sure that this popular person and you could truly be friends is to think about the way the two of you feel and act when you are together. Does the friendship feel good or doesn't it? Are you behaving like the real you or aren't you? Attention is nice—but only when it comes from the right people.

If you pursue a friendship with kids from the popular crowd, will you have to change in any way? In order to fit in, will you have to look different, act different, or stop doing things you enjoy? To help you answer these questions consider these possibilities:

◆ Would you have to change the way you dress?
◆ Would you have to stop playing racquetball and take up tennis?
◆ Would you have to be brash instead of behaving in your naturally quiet way?

The desire to fit in can be intense, but being anything other than oneself rarely leads to happiness or true confidence. It's easy to get swept away in our desire to be a part of something exciting. A little change here, a little change there . . . it hardly seems to matter. But it *does* matter. Because every time you laugh at something you don't really think is funny, wear an outfit that doesn't suit your figure or your personality, or take up a new sport and stop playing one that you enjoy, you are giving up something very important— yourself. By giving up what comes to you naturally and with great ease, you are giving up the things that make you uniquely you. How can that possibly lead to anything good?

You've looked at yourself and the people around you. Now dream up a perfect day to be spent with the people you'd most like to be with, feeling the way you most like to feel. Paint the scene. Live it for a few moments. Now step away and consider the different elements of the dream. Did you have to manipulate anything to make it work? How much of what you know to be true did you have to change in order to make the dream flow?

♦ Did you change people's personalities?
♦ Did you imagine yourself acting in a way in which you know you are not capable?
♦ Did you find it necessary to keep some faces hazy?
♦ What were you doing and/or talking about and were you doing or talking about it with anyone incapable of or uninterested in that kind of activity or conversation?

The object of this final exercise is to determine the distance between your fantasy and reality. Remember that the truth can be wonderful, too. But in order to explore the things and people that *could* be splendid, you have to see the dream for what it is.

If you had to change people's personalities, then perhaps the people you wish to be with have not yet shown you, and may in fact not possess, the qualities you need in a friend in order to feel happy.

If you had to act in a way you know does not come naturally, then maybe you are striving toward something that is bound to leave you feeling left out and lonely.

Did you need to keep some faces hazy in your fantasy? That could mean that you have yet to find people with whom you can really enjoy yourself. It might also mean you do know these people but are reluctant to let them get close to you. Perhaps you are resisting them because they are not from the popular crowd.

Consider what you were doing and with whom. Is this a realistic combination? If so, terrific. If not, you may need to focus more attention on yourself. Perhaps you are concentrating too much on what's "in" instead of what feels good to you. Or perhaps you are in touch with the things that mean a lot to you but are rather confused about how to get them.

And finally if anything really big had to be different— either in you or other people—in order to make the scene work, it's an indication that you need to work on gaining some respect for who you are. After all, what is the problem with the *true* scene? Certainly in a dream scene you are allowed to embellish a bit. Everything can be more glorious than it is in real life. But if you did more than that—if you changed black and white facts to suit your fantasy—maybe you are ignoring what's special about you and what you really need.

Fantasies can be useful. They can inspire us to move forward, to take chances, to believe in ourselves. But they can also be a little dangerous because their beauty can blind us to some important facts about who we are and what we really need.

Everyone needs good, solid friendships. Unfortunately not everyone knows how to get them. That is what the next chapter is all about.

CONFIDENCE BUILDERS
▲▼▲

Most of this chapter has been devoted to the idea that you must be realistic about yourself and those around you in order to find relationships that really work, but there is one point that still needs to be made.

Sometimes, it is within your power to bring out new, desirable aspects of your personality. Perhaps in your fantasy scene you heard yourself laughing happily and telling jokes even though in real life you're usually too uncomfortable to do this. Well, perhaps there is a humorist inside you, but fear has kept your humor hidden. There are ways to let the secret you step forward.

ACT THE WAY YOU WANT TO FEEL

Pretending to feel a certain way sometimes helps you actually start feeling that way. This is partly because people will respond to you differently. If you act as if you are in a terrific mood, more people will want to be near you. As you see this happen, your own mood may begin to lighten. Soon you will probably feel as good as you pretended to feel. Of course there is no need to act like anyone other than yourself. If you want to appear relaxed and happy, do so in your own way. Just because Judith circulates around the room with an eternal giggle does not mean you should do the same. A warm smile or humorous remark now and then will work nicely, too. Do what works for you. It will be much more effective, and it's far easier to keep up when you actually do start feeling good!

DON'T COMPARE, GET INSPIRED

There will always be someone who is smarter, prettier, handsomer, more athletic, or more talented than you. This is true for everyone—popular people included.

Instead of comparing yourself to others, which will only leave you feeling lacking, why not get inspired? If Jyl's English papers always get As but yours do not, don't give up. Set up a meeting with your teacher and ask her how you can improve your work. If Jason continually beats your record at track, work harder on your own performance. Concentrate on bettering your numbers. Discovering that you're improving steadily will give you a real lift. Focusing on Jason's success will not. When you see someone do something terrific, don't say, "Boy. I could never do that." Instead, applaud and say, "That was terrific. What could I get good at?" or, "How could I learn from what I just saw? I'd love to improve."

FIVE

FRIENDSHIPS— THE ONLY POPULARITY THAT REALLY COUNTS

▲▼▲

atching a popular crowd from afar might make you feel a twinge of loneliness or even helplessness, as if having friends is a talent to which only some people can lay claim. Nothing could be further from the truth. Having friends is not a talent. It is not a gift that only some people are born with. It is a *skill*. And a skill is something anyone can learn.

There are a lot of misconceptions about friendships. People think friends are easy to come by. Not so. It isn't easy to find people with whom we are compatible. We all have different ideas about what is right, wrong, fun, fair, upsetting, maddening, and so on. Sometimes it's very hard to find people with whom we fit comfortably.

People think friendships are easy to keep. Again, not so. Life can be very difficult. We all have to face problems that could test our friendships in many ways. We may, because of

41

trying circumstances, behave selfishly or lose our temper. Likewise, we may be treated cruelly or unfairly by friends who are going through their own tough times. Sometimes it is hard to give friends what they deserve and, at the same time, satisfy our own needs.

Many people think good friends will always enjoy one another. This is impossible! We all lead separate lives and have different problems and responsibilities. Sometimes they will clash. Arguments will occur, and we have to weather them. Sometimes a friend who is having serious troubles may depress us. Still, though it isn't fun, we have to stand by that person's side. That is part of friendship, too.

Finally, one of the biggest misconceptions about friendships is that they simply happen. They take no particular thought or effort, but rather simply blossom in the lives of people who have that special magic. Thinking this way leads you into a very unfortunate trap. If you spend your time worrying that you don't have what it takes to form close friendships, you probably won't. It takes two caring people who are willing to make an effort for friendship to blossom.

Making friends is well within your control. You simply have to recognize your own power. You have to find a way to make friendships happen.

This chapter will cover three important topics: how to make friends, how to keep friends, and what to be aware of when befriending popular kids. It's not that the how-to's of making friends with those kids you so admire are any different. They aren't. But you may be different. Lots of kids report that when they find themselves getting friendly with the popular crowd they do and say things they would not ordinarily do and say. They also often admit they don't try to get to know the popular kids on as meaningful a level as they do their other friends.

Making friends takes effort, time, and attention. You need to bring your whole self to the task. Being popular or following a popular person takes effort, too. And the results can often be great fun. But if your goal is building relationships in which you can be yourself, feel cared for, and have a genuinely good time, then first you have to find people with whom you comfortably fit. If they happen to be popular, great!

HOW TO MAKE FRIENDS
▲▼▲

In order to form friendships you have to keep one basic thing in mind, and it's very simple: you have to behave as if you want them.

People do not assume you are interested in pursuing a friendship. Everyone else is just as afraid of being rejected as you are. Even popular kids! Don't expect people to read your mind. They need to sense your openness and interest. Even the most popular people are sometimes hampered by that tiny insecure voice that says, "Maybe this person won't like me."

So make yourself clear. Of course, you needn't march over to someone and say, "Hi! You look interesting so I thought we could be friends." Not everyone is going to respond positively to your overtures, and that kind of aggressive approach could make people feel terribly pressured! But a nice subtle readable message will do the trick. There are lots of people out there who would welcome a friendship with you. Why not make the first move?

LOOK APPROACHABLE

No one feels comfortable approaching a person who seems uptight, uninterested in talking, or depressed. People don't want to be rejected or made to feel awkward, so they usually choose to stay away. It's a natural reaction. It's hard enough starting a conversation with someone we hardly know. Why chance it with someone who seems likely to say, "Go away. I'm not in the mood!"

Imagine you are a new person in school and you are standing in a crowded room. Perhaps a meeting or social event is about to start. If you want to appear approachable keep these pointers in mind:

- Look around the room as if you are interested. This makes it clear that you are open and happy to be there.
- Don't stand in a corner or against a wall. Separating yourself from the crowd in this fashion will make others think that you want to be left alone or that you don't feel you have much to offer.
- Try to keep yourself from stiffening up. Keep your shoulders relaxed and your hands casually at your sides. Your body says a lot. A stiff stance will say, "I am uncomfortable here." That is not a very inviting message, and people are likely to stay away.
- Don't stand in a huddle with one or two friends. People don't like to interrupt what appears to be an intimate conversation. It takes nerve to approach another person. They need to feel fairly confident that if they do, they will be welcomed. Two or three people with their heads together is definitely not an open invitation!
- If you see someone who looks interesting studying you, smile. You may feel safer looking distant, as if you don't care, but that will intimidate this stranger! If you catch someone's eye, look friendly and smile. It's a way of saying, "I'm open to you." And if that person doesn't approach you, don't panic. You can handle it. All you did was smile. That was nice of you. It's the other person's loss.

ACT INTERESTED

One of the best ways to draw others in is to make your interest in them quite clear. People feel flattered when their views or ideas are appreciated. Letting them know you find them attractive or interesting goes a long way toward creating the right atmosphere for friendship.

♦ If you see someone who looks interesting, walk over, introduce yourself, and ask a question. Questions help to get conversations moving. They give your partner something to tell you and you something to learn.

♦ Be a detective. As you are talking, look and listen for clues. Has this person said something that could be the subject of an entire conversation? Is he or she holding or wearing something you could talk about?

Steve was standing by himself in his homeroom feeling terribly lonely. The bell was not due to ring for another five minutes, and the room was slowly filling up. Suddenly he saw a friendly looking boy walk in and stand by the window. He was carrying a sketchpad. Gathering up all his courage, Steve approached him. "Hello," he said. "My name is Steve. Are you taking an art course? I like to paint, too."

The boy studied Steve for a moment and then broke into a huge smile. "Yeah?" He laughed. "Well, I hope you're better at it than I am!"

Steve shook his head and smiled back. "I didn't say I was good. I just said I liked to paint."

The boy stuck out his hand. "Paul here," he offered.

♦ Concentrate when people are talking to you. Nothing turns people off more than talking to someone whose mind is elsewhere. If you want to befriend a person, make it clear you are all there.

Don't look around the room.
Keep your eyes on your partner's face.
Don't restlessly shift positions a hundred times in one minute.
Ask questions about the subject at hand.
Don't switch subjects because the current one is not all that interesting to you.

♦ Respect the privacy of this new person you are attempting to befriend. No matter how anxious you might be to plunge in, remember a certain distance is important. People don't like to feel crowded, as if you want more from them than they are ready or willing to give. Keep your questions and comments easy and relaxed, and stick to subjects that are not too personal. You might be anxious to make a new friend, but both of you need time to learn to trust each other.

♦ Make sure the conversation is not one-sided. No one likes to listen to people who talk about themselves all the time. On the other hand, they don't want to disclose all sorts of things about their own lives while you keep quiet about yourself. When you are talking with someone new, it's important to share information. It's a risk each of you must take in order to set the stage for growing closer.

♦ Feel free to issue the first invitation. Lots of people would rather not make an overture because they fear rejection. If two people are in a panic about being turned down, how will they ever get together?

♦ If you would like to approach a very popular person, go ahead! We've already discovered that lots of popular people would like to meet new kids, but because of the crowd they travel in, they often fail to do so. Well, help them out. Wait for a moment when he or she is not surrounded by friends and walk over. Start a conversation the same way you would with anyone else.

Judy, tray in hand, stood looking out over the large school cafeteria. Her eyes settled on Lia's table. She was sitting with her friends having what appeared to be a very lighthearted conversation. Just that morning Lia had made a joke as she and Judy stood side by side at their lockers. Judy had laughed out loud. There was something about Lia she'd always liked, but she was just too intimidated to pursue a friendship. Awkwardly, Judy stood there another moment or two and then finally walked toward the table of very popular girls. As she approached, several of the girls stopped talking, and Judy swallowed hard. Suddenly Lia turned around, saw Judy standing there, and said, "Oh, hi! Sit down!" Judy flashed her a grateful smile and happily took a seat.

Lia may know she is popular. But that doesn't mean she thinks everyone likes her. Popular people need clues that you are interested, just like anyone else.

BEING A GOOD FRIEND
▲▼▲

Friendships need attention. The biggest mistake people make once they establish a friendship is that they take it for granted. They assume it will always be there, no matter what. Well, it may not.

Friends rely on one another to meet their mutual needs. Of course none of us can meet every expectation others have of us, but if we regularly come through in most ways, the friendship will grow stronger and stronger.

Here, then, is a guide to keeping your friendships on the right track despite any wrong turns both of you may occasionally make.

TAKE THE TIME TO REALLY LISTEN

Friends need to know you are there for them. Sometimes they will tell you exactly what they need. They may say, "Please come over right now! I feel terrible!" But other times they may not. They may simply hope or expect that you will know how they are feeling and want to help. In truth, there will be times when you miss the boat...when you simply don't pick up on the fact that a friend needs your help in some way. But if you take the time to listen, not just to your friends' words but to their tone of voice as well, you should do fine. Trust your instincts. Pay attention to those words that may go unspoken but that hang in the air nonetheless.

Friends also need to know you want to hear what they have to say—that you are interested in their ideas, experiences, and concerns. They need to trust that your mind won't wander and that you will offer clear, careful feedback—not impulsive remarks just to speed up the conversation. If a friend tells you a story that you can relate to, it is much smarter to say, "That happened to me once. I felt very strange. How do you feel?" rather than, "Oh, listen to what happened to me! You won't believe it!" Your friend might be interested in your story, but not until he or she has had a chance to air his or her feelings.

Good friends give one another the attention they need.

BE OPEN-MINDED

People don't like to be judged. They don't like to feel that if they do or think something unusual they will be ignored or criticized or teased. If a friend has an opinion that you don't like, it doesn't make her wrong. It makes her different from you. Her feelings and ideas deserve respect even if they don't match yours. "I wouldn't feel that way, but if you do you must have your reasons" is a much more open-minded and non-judgmental comment than "I can't believe you think that! Are you nuts?" Friends need to know that you will accept them as they move through their lives, learning and growing. Part of learning and growing is experimenting. Trying new activities, feeling new emotions, and developing new beliefs are part of the process of growing up. Friends need to be able to discuss these changes without sitting in judgment upon each other as the changes occur.

Friends who allow for each other's differences usually, ironically, grow closer together.

~~Don't~~ BE RELIABLE

Your friends need to know they can count on you. As noted earlier, there will be times when you can't meet every need. Still it's important to be a person people feel they can count on. If you make plans to do something, stick to them. If you have begun holding your friend's hand through a particular problem, continue to do so. You may not be able to comfort or support your friend every moment, but you should stick by him or her as much as possible. Not just when it fits your schedule. Not just when you are in the mood. Be there when your friend needs you, so that he or she can rely on you. This kind of support will not be forgotten. Lending your concern even when you are not in the mood will serve to create an extremely solid friendship.

HAVE REASONABLE EXPECTATIONS OF YOUR FRIENDS

Friends are just people. They have weaknesses and strengths. Occasionally they will hurt or disappoint us, not because they don't care, but because they have their own needs and desires, which might conflict with ours. It's important to give each other room to separate and not be together every moment.

Also, don't expect to get back exactly what you give to a particular friend. Again, everyone is different. You may be able to listen for hours on end to your girlfriend's problem, but that doesn't mean she can do the same for you. On the other hand, perhaps she has a knack for picking out a funny card or a small gift that really does cheer you up. We all are particularly good at certain aspects of friendship. Some of us are very good at being nonjudgmental. Others are fabulous listeners. Some may be great at cheering people up and making them laugh, while others are terrific motivators who can get their friends out of a rut in no time.

It's important to concentrate on your friends' strengths and to understand what you can and cannot expect from them. (Of course if you are consistently unhappy or disappointed with a friend, he or she may not be the right person for you.) It is wise to build relationships with more than one person. All of us have complicated needs that can never be met by just one person. If you feel very satisfied most of the time, you are very lucky. And you'll be luckier still if your friends tolerate your weaknesses just as well!

BE HONEST BUT TACTFUL

Honesty builds trust. It also sometimes hurts. Your friend might feel slighted, offended, hurt, shocked, unhappy, or betrayed. But most often, once you discuss your views, these difficult feelings will soften and you will be left with something very nice—the certainty that you can trust each other to speak your mind.

That brings us to the subject of tact. You do not need to blurt out the truth in painful detail. There are ways to get a point across so as to make it easier to hear. If the goal of honesty is to help someone, you will want to express yourself in a thoughtful, gentle manner. That way, your friend will find it easier to hear the truth without getting defensive. If you speak your mind with no sensitivity, your friend might be too busy defending himself to gain anything from the conversation. It is not necessary to say, "You cheated off me on that test, and I resent it. Why don't you study for once?" when you can just as easily say, "I studied hard for that test, and I felt upset when I realized you were copying my answers. If you need help next time, please ask me beforehand. I'll help you study."

Even though people prefer to hear what they want to hear, they can still tell when someone is not being honest. Most people know the truth somewhere inside themselves. If you consistently just say what you know people want to hear, pretty soon no one will listen. So say what you think, but say it with care and thought. You may have to deal with a flash of temper, but in the long run you will still have a very good friend.

GET ANGRY—REASONABLY

Anger is a very difficult emotion. It has the power to wipe out all the good feelings you have for another person. It can make you do and say things that you might later regret and, even worse, things others might never forget.

No honest relationship can exist without some angry moments. They arise because two different people with two different sets of needs and desires find themselves in a situation wanting very different things. They will hurt, annoy, or disappoint each other, and tension will mount. It feels awful, but it's not a bad thing.

If you are angry with each other and face it honestly, the two of you could emerge from the confrontation even better friends than before. Trust develops when two people can honestly state how they feel and know that the other cares enough to listen and to try to reach a compromise or a new understanding. The presence of anger, after all, does not mean the absence of caring. In fact, it means quite the opposite. We tend to get the angriest at people who matter to us the most!

In dealing with anger it is important to follow some very clear guidelines. An angry moment well handled brings people together. An angry moment mishandled will only tear them apart.

♦ Keep your voice calm. An irritated or loud voice will immediately put your friend on the defensive. He'll be so busy worrying about how to stick up for himself that he won't even hear what you are saying.

♦ Don't accuse. Instead, explain how you feel. If someone has hurt you, don't say, "You are unbelievably selfish!" Rather, say something like "I felt terrible when you did

that. I felt as if you weren't thinking about me at all."
This will help your friend focus on how she has affected
you rather than on the hurtful things you are thinking
about her.

♦ Keep your complaint limited to the immediate event.
Don't drag up past grudges. Don't say things like
"You've done this before. Remember when...?" or
"And by the way, when you made that comment last
week about my grades, I was really mad then, too." This
does nothing but make it hard to pay attention to the
real and current problem. The person who has offended
you will be so busy trying to remember past events that
he won't have time to focus on the situation at hand and
to attempt a resolution.

♦ Don't walk off, slam doors, or hang up. If necessary,
agree to continue another time. Sometimes in the middle of a difficult angry conversation you or your friend
might feel like simply walking away. One or both of you
could become so upset that you feel the only thing to do
is deliver the ultimate insult—the turned back. When
people suddenly turn and walk away, slam a door, or
hang up the phone, they are saying, "I don't want to
talk with you anymore, and I don't care how you feel
about it." This is a big mistake. It can be very difficult
to walk back, open the door, or pick up the phone once
more. Instead, if your emotions are getting out of control, say something like this: "I am so angry I'm afraid I
might do or say something I don't really mean. Let's
continue this another time when we are calmer." This
communicates two important things—the extent of your
anger and your concern for the relationship. It's a caring
message, and it should set you up for a thoughtful
conversation later on when you are more in control.

♦ Listen to the other side. When you are upset or feel as if
you are being attacked, it's very tempting to concentrate only on what you think. Don't do it! Your friend is
angry or defensive for her own reasons. Some of her
feelings might be very valid. Express your respect for

who she is by considering her point of view. You might learn something that will lessen your anger. Sometimes people are unwilling to listen to the other side because they are afraid of being proven wrong. Unfortunately, they often miss the opportunity to reach a new understanding with a good friend that could leave both people feeling better about each other than before.

♦ Understand that not all arguments have an easy resolution. Sometimes you and your friend will have to agree to disagree. There are times when each of you may have an important point, or because of your personalities one of you may simply be unable to agree with the other's perception of a situation. If there are enough strong elements to your friendship, and if each of you feels that the other has tried to listen and resolve the problem, you may have to let the argument go—in other words, forget about it. People don't need to agree on everything to be good friends. In fact, since friends are supposed to be able to learn from each other and broaden each other's views, disagreements are very useful. They are the springboards for developing new views!

KEEP ALL OF YOUR FRIENDS IN MIND

It's fun to have lots of friends. That way there's always someone with whom to do things. But it's tricky, too. No one likes to become a victim of the "out of sight, out of mind" syndrome. In other words, just because you are spending the afternoon with one friend doesn't mean you have to put your other friends completely out of your head. Suppose just the day before one close buddy told you a sad story. Now you've just finished spending the afternoon with another friend, and you're exhausted. You'd like to just eat dinner and watch TV. It would be thoughtful and loyal to call that troubled friend to see how he's doing first. You needn't stay on the phone for hours. A simple brief conversation will show him that he is on your mind.

Friends have to recognize that they do not own each other. There are other people in their lives, and they have to make room for everyone. Feelings may get hurt. Disappointment may, at times, flourish. But if we do our best to remember that we don't exist in separate little boxes and that we are constantly affecting one another, even when we are not in the same room, we can usually muddle through. Even the smallest gesture of recognition or reaching out can go a long way toward letting people know we care.

All of these elements play a strong part in creating solid friendships. Consistency, honesty, openness, reasonable expectations, and a careful handling of anger will create an atmosphere of respect and caring between friends. You can bring these qualities to a friendship. Doing so will undoubtedly build your circle of friends. It may even bring you that magical thing called popularity for which you've been aching. But of course it isn't popularity or even magic that will leave you feeling terrific. Having good true friends will do that.

BEFRIENDING THE POPULAR CROWD
▲▼▲

Popular people, as we've already discussed, are just like everyone else. They need the same things from a good friendship as you do. In fact, the only thing that may be different about a friendship with a popular person is you!

Karen felt terrific. She was hanging out with Zoe and her friends. They'd actually invited her to go with them to a party and have a sleep-over afterward. She'd felt bad telling her good friend Patti that she wouldn't be spending the night with her, but then, Karen told herself, we can't do everything together. She walked

*over to the refreshment table at the party and poured
herself a glass of soda.*

*Suddenly Zoe called out, "Karen! Bring me one, too,
okay?" Karen nodded happily and poured another
glass.*

*"Karen," a friend of Zoe's chimed in, "bring one for
me and Debbie, too." Again Karen nodded. But of
course when she tried to carry the drinks back she
couldn't manage.*

*"Someone has to help me," she said loudly in her
new friends' direction.*

*"There's a tray under the table," Zoe responded with
a big warm smile, then turned back to the tête-à-tête she
was having with her pals.*

*For a moment Karen almost blurted out, "Get it
yourself," but something stopped her. The fear of leaving
the popular crowd before she'd even had a chance to
really move in was just too much for her. Unhappily she
bent and peered under the table.*

Sometimes finally becoming friends with a popular crowd
or person can seem like a dream come true. We don't want to
let the dream go, and so we may try everything within our
power to keep it going. In the process, we can easily lose sight
of our beliefs, our needs, and our desires. We may even alter
our natural and understandable reactions to things, much as
Karen did. When this happens, we are doing ourselves and
our new friends a disservice. As soon as we start denying who
we really are, the less honest we become about how we feel.
Hiding from one's feelings can bring unhappiness and tension into a relationship.

By trying to be the person we think others want us to be,
we fail to give ourselves the opportunity to be liked for who
we are. It is a wonderful feeling to let others experience our
real selves and to be liked for it! (Perhaps Zoe would have
been impressed if Karen had insisted that she was not a
waitress!)

At the same time, we aren't giving the popular person a chance to be liked for who he or she really is. We are so involved with our fantasies about her and what we are sure she would like us to be that we don't even stop to get to know the real person. The result? She never gets to know us and we never get to know her. We're busy being what we think she wants, and she's busy playing the role she perceives everyone expects of her! What a dismal cycle!

If you want to be a member of a popular crowd, the first and most important thing you have to remember is that it won't work unless you act like yourself. Otherwise the relationships will be superficial at best and hurtful at worst. And in the process you could lose a great number of the good friendships you have formed outside of this seemingly exciting crowd.

So the next time you find yourself happily getting close to a popular crowd or person, keep these thoughts in mind:

- ◆ At some point I'm not going to be able to act the way I think they expect me to, so I might as well find out right now if they can appreciate me as I really am.
- ◆ Doing everything that others want me to do will not make them like me. It will only encourage them to come to me when they want something.
- ◆ Most people know the truth. If I compliment and reassure them too much, I might think I'm winning their affection, but I'm only going to win their distrust.
- ◆ People have more going on inside them than meets the eye. Maybe if I speak the truth about how I feel, I'll find out something new and interesting about these popular kids that will leave me feeling a lot more comfortable with them.
- ◆ If I am laughed at, teased, or treated cruelly when I say how I really feel, I will know these people are not for me. It has nothing to do with their popularity. I could get along fine with other people who are popular. But these

particular people and I are not a good match.

Good friends are invaluable. Everyone, popular or not, needs friendship and has the capacity to make it happen. No one moves through this life without some feelings of loneliness and rejection. But we all deserve and need a sense of belonging and the feeling that people out there really care.

So the next time you find yourself wishing you had more friends, go out and do something about it. And the next time you feel yourself gazing with envy at those who seem to have more friends than they can manage, remember that everything is not always as it seems. And if you feel the urge to get closer to those popular people, do yourself and them a favor. Remember who you are, give them a chance to be who they really are, and then decide if you want the friendship—in that exact order please!

CONFIDENCE BUILDER
▲▼▲

Friends are a wonderful resource. They are fun companions and also important reality testers and ego reinforcers. What does this mean? It means they can tell you how things really are when you are too emotional to see straight. And they can remind you of all the terrific things you have going for you when you are feeling too low to believe in yourself.

INTERVIEW YOUR FRIENDS

Ask your friends what they see in you. It sounds silly, and maybe even a bit embarrassing, but try not to feel that way. As soon as your friends are through answering your question, they will more than likely want to know what you like about them! In case you think this is just too awkward for words, here are two examples of how to pull it off.

- "I feel terrible today. Could you tell me why you like me so much? I might just believe you!"
- "I'm angry at myself. Last week I felt good, and now I can't even remember why. Could you please remind me what I have going for me? I can't think of a thing."

SIX

POPULARITY AND ROMANCE

▲▼▲

Everyone wants to be popular with people of the opposite sex.

Very few, however, attract as many members of the opposite sex as they would like. When someone does, most often it is because he or she suits the current ideal of what is beautiful or sexy. It would be foolish to imply that it isn't fun to have those much admired looks. It does guarantee lots of positive attention.

But it doesn't guarantee love. While there are people out there who easily get dates because of their looks or their flirtatious ways, true romance does not necessarily follow. And it is for the same reason that we discussed earlier in the friendship chapter. True romance or true love has to do with more than looks and images. It has to do with genuine caring.

Feeling many pairs of admiring eyes on you is certainly fun and flattering. But a mutual attraction with just one person is where the real excitement lies. You may think this hard to believe, but feeling people gaze at you longingly only feeds your ego. Experiencing the thrill of caring for and wanting to be close to someone who feels the same way about you offers so much more.

Looks can attract, but they can't capture. They can make people pay attention, but they can't make them care. Besides, many things other than looks come into play when the game of who-attracts-whom begins. And in the end it's the whole picture that will really count when it comes to building a full relationship.

HOW DOES ATTRACTION WORK?
▲▼▲

Most people are a mixture of very attractive and not so attractive attributes. Just as they have positive and negative character traits, they have positive and negative physical traits as well.

Fortunately for all of us, it is the whole picture that people see. In fact, different people see that whole picture in very different ways. What's very attractive to one person may be only marginally so to another. What may strike one person as rather ordinary may seem beautiful to another person.

There are many reasons why different people will see the same person in different ways. One reason has no clear explanation. Why does one person love blue while another prefers red? The answer remains unclear. Perhaps we develop particular preferences for things because of past experiences we can barely remember, or simply in response to those elements of our character that make us unique. An adventurous person, for example, might prefer an unusual-looking person to a classic beauty.

Another reason has to do with whether a person reminds us of someone we love or admire. Perhaps you've always thought your short, blond, athletic brother is the greatest. You may find yourself attracted to short blond athletes. Perhaps someone reminds you of a movie star on whom you have an immense crush. A person who reminds you of that star will easily garner your attention.

Then there is the matter of what we read into looks. If you think broad shoulders and large, warm, sympathetic eyes indicate that a person is both masculine and sensitive then, at least at first, you will feel attracted to such a person. If you assume that a very tall guy with a shy smile must be insecure, you may not feel attracted to him at all—at first, that is. But once you get to know him you may discover traits you hadn't expected.

This brings us to a very critical factor in why a person is or is not attracted to another: personality. After the first glance (or the first date), one of the most powerful determinants of how attractive you will look to another person has to do with your personality and the feelings it inspires. Your personality is reflected in the expression in your face, the way you stand, the way you move, the things you say, the way you laugh, and even the way you listen to another person. When people see you, they are looking not just at your appearance but also at the "feel" of you.

It works like this. Initially you may not think someone is particularly attractive. All you see is a very large nose and frizzy hair. But if the individual's personality appeals to you, that large nose may become overshadowed by a beautiful smile. The frizzy hair may seem to go well with a pair of gorgeous green eyes. In other words, someone's personality can influence what you see.

The ability to attract is something to which everyone can lay claim. It rests in our uniqueness. You don't need to be popular to experience a mutual attraction.

It is very easy to look at those people who are popular with the opposite sex and think, "If only I looked like that..." But it's critical to remember that you have your own statement to make. Plenty of people are quite attractive and still do not inspire the interest of others. It's one thing to gaze with admiration at someone. It's another thing to want to be with that person all of the time.

MYTHS ABOUT POPULAR PEOPLE AND ROMANCE
▲▼▲

Popular kids always seem to have someone special. It doesn't matter that their relationships don't last very long.

Having a boyfriend or a girlfriend or a date every Saturday night seems like a fabulous fact of their lives...one that we would give anything to attain.

In Chapter Two we explored the myths about popularity. Now let's look at three common myths about popular people and romance. Not only will this discussion help you be less envious, it should also help you be less demanding of yourself. Having crushes, risking your emotions, trusting, and reaching out can be terribly scary for anyone in a romantic relationship. You are not the only one who suffers through the mixed-up feelings of tremendous excitement, insecurity, and hurt.

MYTH #1: POPULAR PEOPLE CAN GET ANYONE THEY WANT

Girls and boys who seem to embody all of the romantic traits we seek in a boyfriend or girlfriend are probably able to attract the interest of many people. But interest is a long way from genuine caring. A beautiful girl may inspire a very handsome guy to ask her out, but it doesn't then follow that he will sincerely care about her. Nor does it follow that, even if he does like her, he won't be interested in dating other girls as well.

Pamela was used to being admired. Her long, thick, dark hair, large, expressive eyes, and curvy figure attracted attention everywhere she went. But right now it did not seem to be doing the trick. She'd gone out to a party the other night with Richard, the most fantastic-looking guy in school. They'd had a good time, too... but now he was flirting with someone else at the football game. Pamela pretended not to notice. She chattered gaily with her friends and began flirting with Stan, who had always liked her and who was sitting to her right. But inside she felt awful. What, she wondered desperately, had she done wrong?

Some popular people not only look great but also have

personalities many people enjoy. They will indeed attract a lot of sincere romantic affections. But even they will not necessarily leave a trail of broken hearts behind them. Everyone's personality is different. Just because someone is very attractive or has a nice personality does not mean that *everyone* will fall in love with him or her. That takes a special connection between two people. It's rare and special and happens no more frequently to popular people than to anyone else.

MYTH #2: POPULAR PEOPLE NEVER GET DUMPED

Someone may be great-looking and have a wonderful personality, but that doesn't mean he or she can retain the interest of others forever. Young people enjoy the excitement of a new romance. It feels thrilling. But after a while, when it loses its newness, one person may want to explore another relationship to see how it feels to be close to someone else. It's not a matter of liking the first person less. It's simply a quest for new excitement and new experiences. Good looks and a sparkling personality are no protection when the need to explore takes hold. Popular people are left behind just as often as those who seem less popular. It may not look that way, because popular people sometimes fight harder to hide the fact, aware that they have an image to protect.

MYTH #3: POPULAR PEOPLE ARE INTERESTED ONLY IN OTHER POPULAR PEOPLE

The only reason that popular people would only be interested in other popular people is out of insecurity. A date with another popular person would confirm their own status. A date with a not-so-popular person would threaten their need to feel important and on top. In other words, wanting to date a popular person has everything to do with proving one's own self-worth and very little to do with any sincere attraction.

That is why it is misguided to feel hurt or slighted when a popular person doesn't seem interested in you. He or she is probably more insecure than you are!

Popular people have many of the same fears as you. They can make their lives look great. It can appear that the world is in love with them. But deep inside they are afraid of being hurt, just like everyone else. And with good reason. They can be hurt just as badly.

HOW NOT TO ATTRACT THE OPPOSITE SEX
▲▼▲

Unfortunately lots of people, in an effort to capture a person or persons they feel attracted to, concentrate almost entirely on being what they think that person would like them to be. It's as if they are saying, "The things that are special about me are simply not special enough. This person's idea of what is good is much better, so I'll try to be that."

It is critical to remember that if someone else has an image of who he or she is attracted to, and it isn't you, that does not make you wrong. It simply makes the two of you not right for each other.

Before we get into what you can do to attract other people, let's consider and then toss out some of the unfortunate things people do in the name of romance. If you take the time to consider the problems each of these approaches might pose, you will be far more open to following a healthier, and ultimately more romantic, route!

SOME PEOPLE PUT ON AN ACT

Everyone at one time or another—in an effort to attract someone—will put on a show. A shy person may attempt to tell jokes. A girl who prefers tailored clothes may suddenly show up in a Madonna outfit. Or a guy anxious to look athletic may join the basketball team. On the surface this seems like a reasonable solution. If you want someone who is attracted to a certain type and you're not it, then why not change?

It doesn't work that way.

Elizabeth couldn't stop thinking about Rick. He was everything she thought was exciting in a guy. He was athletic, smart, dark, tall, and confident. The only problem was that Rick seemed to go for girls very unlike Elizabeth. He seemed to like very feminine girls who were also athletic. It didn't seem to matter how smart they were as long as they were into sports. His last girlfriend was on the tennis team.

Elizabeth was an excellent student, not terribly athletic, and very feminine in her own special way. Her figure was rather nice and she enjoyed pretty clothes, but lace, pink, and tiny jewelry were not her style. Still, she was determined to win Rick over, and so she began showing up at school in soft pastel colors, wearing ribbons in her hair, and raising her hand less often in class. It felt awful. For one thing, Elizabeth was sure she looked better in strong colors such as royal blue. She much preferred wearing her thick pretty hair in a French braid, and it was hard for her not to be more active in class. It felt good to be prepared and knowledgeable. Besides, while Rick did take the time to flirt with her a bit during one lunch period, their relationship had gone absolutely nowhere. Shortly thereafter Elizabeth went back to the way she really was. She still had a crush on Rick, though, so she halfheartedly tried out for the girls' softball team. It was a fiasco. And then she met Kevin who, it turned out, liked smart girls.

You may not, on occasion, be able to resist the temptation to change—to make yourself into someone you definitely are not. On rare occasions you may discover hidden talents as you travel down an unfamiliar road, but most times you will be heading for frustration. Perhaps Elizabeth, at this time in Rick's life, simply wasn't the kind of girl he was after. In a way she was insulting Rick by assuming that if he saw a pastel ribbon he would fall in love.

That brings us to the most basic piece of faulty reasoning that leads people to try to change. In an effort to figure out why someone is not interested in us, we tend to break the problem down into pieces we can understand. "It's just that I'm not as funny as Sean." "If only I were as athletic as Gail." "I'm going to try and be as lively and upbeat as Jayne."

But that's not how it works. People are attracted to the whole person. We have also learned they are drawn to people for unconscious reasons. Simply changing our hairstyle or pretending to have a particular talent will not necessarily draw anyone to us. The truth is we might as well keep our own style and encourage those people who find it attractive.

SOME PEOPLE IGNORE THEIR BELIEFS

In an effort to capture someone's heart, we may be tempted to behave in ways with which we are not totally comfortable.

We may say things we don't mean. We might pretend to believe in things that in fact mean nothing to us. And we may actually do things that are not simply awkward but also quite hurtful. All in the name of winning someone's heart.

But winning someone over is never, in this situation, the only goal. When people are willing to put aside what they believe in to attract someone else it can't simply be "for love." After all, true love can never blossom between two people who are lying about very fundamental things. When people turn their backs on their own important belief systems, it is their own insecure needs, not their aching hearts, that motivate them.

> *Lisa could not get Dennis out of her mind. He was not her usual type. He was much wilder than the guys she usually liked. But he was also incredibly cute, and all her friends had a crush on him. She also realized*

she was probably a bit too straight for him. His last girlfriend had been a girl from the neighboring town who had a reputation for being pretty wild herself. Used to attracting almost any guy she liked, Lisa became progressively more worried that Dennis was not interested. She worried, in fact, that she was completely losing her sex appeal. And so, despite her discomfort, she stopped hanging out at her spot and started frequenting his—the local video arcade. He and his friends hung out there telling loud jokes and flirting. Shortly after Lisa began to spend time there, Dennis started to give her the eye. She was thrilled. Then one afternoon he wandered over and asked her if she'd like to go back to his house with his friends and party. She was worried. Dennis seemed to move at a pace that was a good deal faster than what she was used to. Still, filled with excitement, she accepted his invitation. No sooner had she walked in the door than the truth of the matter hit hard. "Here," Dennis said, handing her a beer. "There's plenty more where this came from." Lisa smiled meekly, took it, and fervently wished she'd never met Dennis.

Ignoring your sense of right and wrong or putting aside rules you usually follow in order to attract someone will never work. Sooner or later you will find yourself in a situation that feels all wrong or, even worse, that could be dangerous. Besides, two people who think quite differently about very important issues will eventually stop enjoying each other's company.

SOME PEOPLE USE PHYSICAL CLOSENESS
▲▼▲

Unfortunately, lots of people think that physical closeness is one way of achieving romantic popularity. They think that if they "do it" they'll have lots of dates, and if they don't they'll be all alone.

But let's explore these assumptions for a moment, because they leave out one very important thing. And that is, *love.*

Sex (to be defined here as any kind of physical closeness) is a big deal to everyone. And when you're first experimenting with it, no matter how "far" you go, it can feel very exciting and extremely urgent. If you offer physical closeness as a possibility and that's what someone wants then you will likely be asked out. But you will not get the one thing you probably want most. Affection.

The truth is, no amount of sex in the world can buy love. It can't even buy a feeling of emotional closeness. It can offer some excitement and the sense that one is attractive. But that's about it.

Likewise, the absence of sex will not keep love away. People truly care about others because of who they are. They express that caring often through sex. But sex itself does not win or lose affection.

So, while it may be difficult to watch someone who frequently shares his or herself physically with others, dating a lot, try and keep a few things in mind.

1) It may look like fun, but that person can be just as lonely as you. In fact perhaps more so. It is very lonely to participate in an act that is supposed to be born of love or affection, but which most certainly is not. It can provoke some very lonely feelings.

2) Saying "no" because you are not ready will not affect how much someone likes you. He or she may be frustrated or even act annoyed. And that *can* feel terrible. But it won't cause someone to care less.

3) Any kind of physical intimacy only feels good if people feel good about it. If you are doing it out of real affection for someone, no matter what amount of physical contact you have, it should feel nice. If you are doing it to keep someone interested, it's not going to feel good to you. And if it doesn't feel good to you, your partner won't truly enjoy it either. So you might as well be true to yourself. That way sex will

remain what it should be—a lovely, exciting, warm experi- ence for both people.

If someone is interested in you for all the right reasons, whether or not you want to increase the physical intimacy will not affect the affection between you. If someone is only interested in you for sex and you say "no," it is likely you won't see that person again.

That's not much of a loss.

Which brings us to the one issue you might have with this approach to sex, dating, and popularity. And that is, "If I won't do it, won't he find someone who will?"

The answer is, he may. But that doesn't mean you should do what doesn't feel right simply to "keep" someone. It won't feel good, and in the end could ruin the relationship.

So in a way, you're trapped. But it's a good trap, because it forces you to choose the road that's right for you. It's the only way to win. If the relationship is good you will give each other the space you need.

One final note strictly from the boy's perspective. There is a myth that boys "should know what to do"—that they should be the more "experienced" one. As a result they often feel as if they have to perform and that if they don't girls will think they are immature. How unfair!

First of all, boys have no obligation to be any better "kissers" than girls. Nor should they have to be any more familiar with how to touch someone with whom they want to be close. Secondly, the pressure to be the one who "knows" can make it terribly difficult for any guy to relax and simply think about how he feels, or whether or not he is comfortable with the degree of intimacy.

The point is, both males and females have anxiety about the physical side of their romantic relationships. Each is often afraid and each needs sensitivity. Neither should have to view sex as the key to caring...and certainly not to popularity!

HOW TO ATTRACT
THE OPPOSITE SEX
▲▼▲

You can make yourself more attractive to the opposite sex. But this only works the way you would like it to if, in the process, you are making yourself more attractive to *you.*

The most foolproof way to attract people to you is to have some faith in yourself. People of the same sex *and* the opposite sex are most attracted to people who believe in and like themselves. When you feel good about yourself you send out this message: "I have a lot going for me." People can sense that and will tend to believe it. It will make them feel excited and happy to be near you.

This doesn't mean, of course, that you can't have your moments of feeling down. We've already discussed how no one likes to be around people who are forever feeling wonderful— as if no problem or insecurity ever touched their lives. That simply isn't real. Still, if you have some faith in yourself and let others see that you find yourself attractive, others will probably feel the same way.

Consider the following pointers for being well liked by the opposite sex:

♦ Be yourself. Allow all of the particulars about you to shine forth. Don't play a role. Trying to be "the funny one" or "the athletic one" will only leave you being less than you are. The people who stand out are the ones who make their own statements.

♦ Be appreciative. Let people know that you think they are special. Laughter at the right moments, sincere flattery, nods of understanding, and careful listening all communicate appreciation. When a person feels appreciated, he feels good not only about himself but about the person he is with. This can easily stir up a mutual attraction. But don't overdo it. Whenever people are overly complimentary or too eager to please, the object of their attentions may feel uncomfortable . . . and, ironically, invisible. When someone insists on seeing us in only the most glowing terms, we tend to feel as if we aren't being seen at all.

♦ Act attracted. Let someone know with your eyes and movements that you like him or her. Use a lot of eye contact. Occasionally reach out and touch his or her arm or shoulder as you speak. Stand closer than you might if you were uninterested in a romantic relationship. But don't overdo it. The object is to let someone know you are interested in this special way so that he or she might feel confident enough to respond in kind. If you are too aggressive, however, you could make a person feel crowded and turned off.

♦ Feel sexy without sex. Give yourself a little credit! You don't need to come on like a love god or goddess to be sexy. A nice smile, a flirtatious remark, and a flattering outfit can all contribute to your sex appeal. They are ways of saying, "I like you. I feel good about myself. Let's enjoy ourselves." Behaving in an obvious sexual fashion—pressing yourself up close to someone or wearing an outfit that reveals entirely too much—will not make you attractive to someone in a more meaningful way. That's up to the real you, and putting on a sexy show will often keep people from ever getting to know who you really are. Besides, to some a sexy act is nothing more than a giant turn-off.

FORGET ABOUT THE MOVIES

Movies are, as you know, usually larger than life. The stories are played out with the kind of drama that never happens offscreen. This is especially true of romantic scenes. Isn't it amazing that the actors seem to know which direction to move their heads so their noses never hit when they kiss? Also they never cough or sneeze when they're in a clinch. And their passionate deep breathing is never interrupted by nervous giggles or uncertain glances.

Surely you've noticed all of this, and you may imagine this is the way romance is supposed to be. Well, forget it. That's the movies. The love scenes you've been watching are the result of hours of rehearsals—something we never get in real life!

The next time you are with someone you care for romantically, try to remember that *real* people are nervous. They are not love machines. Some kisses are relaxed, and some aren't. Some handholding is spontaneous and easy, but some produces sweaty palms. And when passion sweeps in, both of you will feel excited, but you will also be uncertain and confused. Remember that you are entitled to express those feelings in words and actions. Human feelings and reactions need not ruin a romantic moment between you and your partner. If you are genuinely attracted to each other that exciting feeling will more than make up for an awkward moment or two. It won't ruin the great romantic scene that both of you expected. In fact, most glitches will go completely unnoticed. And if they are a bit obvious, they might even be considered—yes—charming.

Everyone wants to be popular with the opposite sex. In fact, we usually want it so badly that at times we may do things that don't feel very good in order to make it happen. The result is that the popularity we achieve is not what we'd hoped it would be.

Popularity with the opposite sex is nice, but being attracted to one person who is also attracted to you is better. Having lots of dates can be fun. But going out with one or two people whom you feel close to and attracted to is warm and exciting.

Remember, true romance is a possibility for everyone, including you—especially if you're true to yourself. If you feel attracted to someone who does not appear interested, give it time. Attraction develops in different ways and at different rates with different people. Keep one important thing in mind about attractions between people: they are not etched in stone. An attraction can suddenly surface when for weeks, months, or years there was no interest at all. Or it can disappear when just yesterday you felt you couldn't live without this person.

It's important not to compare yourself to people who have a different date every night. You don't know what goes on during those dates. You only know what it looks like to you. Instead, concentrate on yourself and on finding the kind of person with whom you can truly enjoy yourself.

It's amazing how one good romance between just two people can make both of them feel like the most popular and attractive people in the whole world.

CONFIDENCE BUILDERS
▲▼▲

When it comes to romance, few people feel completely confident. We are vulnerable when we care for someone in a special way. But we all have to take the risk. After all, even though we may be opening ourselves up for hurt we are also giving ourselves a chance to experience some wonderful emotions. The trick is to brave the romantic waters with the idea that you can survive even the worst storm. And always remember that you needn't do everything right in order to make the relationship work.

DON'T OVERPROTECT YOURSELF

Test your strength. Don't be so afraid of getting hurt. Everyone is a fool for love sometimes. People survive. Feelings can grow so intense that you may put your better sense aside and do or say things that put you in a very painful position. It happens to everyone. The best thing to do when this happens is try to learn something from the experience, and remind yourself that you're only human.

Whether you go too far or not, chances are you can take whatever hurt may come your way. Certainly the recovery isn't fun. But you *will* recover, and when you come through the bad feelings, you will be much stronger. It's better to go out there and take a chance on relationships that may not work than to hide from them, afraid of being turned down. You could protect yourself right out of every wonderful feeling a romance can offer. And your confidence in your attractiveness will build a lot faster if you move through a relationship or two that falls apart than if you never form any at all.

SEVEN

THE SHYNESS FACTOR

————————————— ▲▼▲ —————————————

A lot of people ache to be popular, but they are hampered by shyness. Shyness affects different people in different ways, but we do know absolutely two things about shyness. One, it is *very* common. Everyone experiences it in some way at some time. Some people simply hide it better than others. Two, it can be controlled.

A shy person usually approaches other people cautiously. He or she may be timid, retiring, and uncomfortable in the presence of others. Of course, this is not true of all shy people. Shyness, in fact, can indicate some very enviable qualities—a fact that we will explore later in this chapter. But for now, let's consider the ways in which shyness can affect people's lives.

On one end there are those who feel most comfortable alone—thinking, studying, or communing quietly with nature. They are known as introverts—people who prefer being alone because they enjoy solitude or they lack social skills and so feel happiest with a small circle of friends.

In the middle are those people who, to varying degrees, feel uncomfortable in only certain situations with particular people. They would describe themselves as social creatures who sometimes, and often unhappily, feel the need to back off or shut down.

*Barbara had always had a lot of friends. She was
very outgoing and had a talent for making people
laugh—except, that is, when she wasn't around her
buddies. Barbara had a fear of going anyplace by herself and not seeing someone she knew. It didn't seem to
matter whether it was the local pizza shop or the library,
places she frequented on a regular basis. If she was not
positive she'd see a friendly face, she didn't want to go.
This didn't cause any problems with her friendships
until one particular night. Her pal Gina wanted to take
Barbara to her camp reunion party so that Barbara
could meet some new people. But Barbara was afraid
that Gina would disappear on her and she'd have to
speak to people she didn't know well. As a result, she
refused to go. Gina took this to mean Barbara didn't
care much about her friends. Their friendship was
never quite the same after that, and Barbara was left
feeling very mixed up.*

Those people who feel very shy only on occasion can hurt
and confuse not only their good friends but themselves as
well.

And at the far end of shyness are those people who
regularly experience fear whenever it's time to socialize. The
urge to run and hide is often so intense that it's difficult to
resist.

As you can see, shyness can appear in very different
forms.

HOW SHYNESS HURTS
▲▼▲

Shyness is a very complicated condition and not one that
should or can be considered good or bad. What matters most
is whether or not your shyness creates difficulties for you. It's
one thing to feel shy. That happens lots of times to everyone.

It's another thing when it stands between you and the things and people you would most like to enjoy. This can pose very painful problems:

- Shyness can make it difficult to meet people, make friends, and join a crowd.
- Shyness can prevent you from stating your true opinion.
- Shyness can prevent you from standing up for yourself and your rights.
- Shyness may keep others from seeing your most positive attributes.
- Shyness can stop you from asking for help.
- Shyness can make it hard to think clearly and positively about any situation.
- Shyness can cause you to worry excessively about yourself and the impression you are making, when you should be using your energy to reach out.
- Shyness can contribute to loneliness and depression.
- Shyness can be misread by others as aloofness, lack of caring, snobbery, and disinterest. This is what happened in the story of Barbara and Gina.

Shyness can be painful even if it is triggered only occasionally and in response to a particular set of circumstances. If we allow shyness to take over, we are no longer ourselves. We retreat. We don't say what we think. Sometimes we don't talk at all. And often we can't even act in ways that would bring us pleasure.

Allison had just started to feel a little comfortable in her new school. It had taken weeks, but finally she was finding it easier to chat with a few classmates in the morning before the bell rang and to put her tray down next to a couple of particularly friendly kids during lunch. But Tuesday afternoon she was thrown into a panic once more. As she was coming down the front steps of the school talking to a very popular girl next to whom she had sat during math class, Allison found

herself being invited out for pizza with the crowd.
Desperate to go, Allison tried to say yes. But she simply
couldn't. What if I go and I have nothing to say? she
thought to herself. I know they'll think I'm a bore. And
so Allison declined, and then she went home and had a
good cry.

Perhaps the reason we turn away from ourselves is that we are too tuned in to ourselves! We can't stop worrying about a long list of concerns that center on us and our potential failings. Do I look okay? Did I say the right thing? What if I embarrass myself? What if they think I'm silly? What if I can't think of a thing to say? What if I'm a bore?

In many ways when we are being shy, we are operating in a self-involved manner. The truth is, nobody is looking at us as critically as we are at that moment, but the feelings of nervousness, embarrassment, and self-consciousness are so intense we may find that hard to believe. Why? Because at the root shyness is low self-esteem. We are afraid to approach others because we fear we are not worthy or able.

Everyone feels shy sometimes. If your shyness has in any way made you unhappy you need to take heed. It's time to take control of your shyness instead of allowing it to control you! This chapter will point the way.

WHEN SHYNESS SHINES
▲▼▲

The first thing to realize about shyness is that it need not be your enemy. Some people naturally have more retiring personalities than others and would rather place themselves in quiet social circumstances than in boisterous ones. Of course, if popularity is your goal anything short of reaching out to everyone is going to feel like a failure. But—and this is key—it might surprise you to know that many popular people are quite retiring! Others may seek them out in preference to their more outgoing counterparts. And for good reason. They have very enviable personal qualities, many of which you probably have as well!

Coming to grips with who you are and seeing the positives in your personality will give whatever shyness you experience a very different feel. Shyness is not necessarily a trap. It can, instead, be put to work for you.

Let's begin by taking a look at some of the words that are used to describe shy people:

Retiring	Modest
Demure	Thoughtful
Unassuming	Polished
Self-effacing	Soft-spoken
Classy	Mysterious

These are hardly traits of which to be ashamed! A shy person is often seen as quite sophisticated and intelligent as well as rather elegant. A quiet, gentle demeanor suggests a very caring and respectable character. Here are some other benefits of being shy:

♦ Shy people can seem quite interesting. Many people are curious about what goes on in the mind of a person who does not "come forth" easily.

♦ Shyness allows a person to stand back and observe before making any moves. No one expects a very active participation, so the shy person can take his or her time without feeling pressured.

♦ Shy people often make terrific listeners, a quality most people value tremendously. After all, many people prefer to talk rather than listen!

♦ Shy people rarely hurt or dominate others the way some more aggressive people might. They are apt to give others much more room to be themselves. As a result their relationships are often more relaxed.

* Shy people can be secure in the knowledge that they will, in all likelihood, never be accused of obnoxious or loud behavior.

Shyness, then, does not have to be a problem. It may simply be who you are and the way you choose to be. Remember, many shy people enjoy popularity! They may not wish to travel with or be followed by a boisterous crowd. But they can enjoy the respect and admiration of lots of kids just the same.

The real issue concerning you and your shyness is how it makes you feel and how it influences your actions. If it makes you unhappy, chances are you will want to do something about it.

OVERCOMING YOUR SHYNESS

Overcoming shyness is a three-step process. First and foremost, you have to give yourself a break. You have to allow yourself to be who you are and stop looking at your shyness as the single most important—not to mention dreadful—thing about you. Second, you have to understand your shyness. When are you shy? In response to what? How exactly do you feel when shyness strikes? And third, you have to practice changing your behavior. The object here is not to become a new you but rather to find the courage to put forth the whole you.

People can change. Often when we are labeled one thing either by ourselves or others, we tend to feel trapped. This is the way we are, period. But this isn't true. Everyone grows. New experiences can bring out all kinds of qualities in your personality. Your shyness may prevent you from participating in new experiences. So you have to make sure you give yourself a chance to grow and give others a chance to see the changes in you.

ACCEPT YOURSELF AS YOU ARE

Since shyness is very closely linked to self-esteem, how you feel about yourself and your shyness plays a big part in the degree of shyness you experience. In Chapter Three we looked at who you really are. Now let's look at ways you might employ to confidently accept who that is.

♦ One method is to give your shyness room. When you have an attack of shyness, accept it without insulting yourself. Don't sit there thinking, "Why is this happening? How come I can't talk? I hate myself. Why won't this go away?" The more you do that, the more agitated you will become. Remind yourself there is nothing wrong with being quiet. It isn't silly or unattractive. Try new, more patient inner thoughts such as "I'm feeling shy now. Okay. It won't kill me. I'd like to talk to everyone, but right now I can't." Keep your shyness in perspective. If you keep it in its place, it will be easier to overcome.

♦ Remember, also, that getting past your shyness will take a while. Don't expect to change overnight and never be shy again. You need to take chances slowly. You will need a number of experiences in which you try on different types of behavior and get positive results before you begin to feel a change. Don't rush the process. If you want to gain control of your shyness, you will have to treat yourself gently. And you will have to realize that just about everyone experiences feelings of shyness now and then. It's not something you can strike from your personality forever. When that uncomfortable feeling creeps over you, don't panic. Remind yourself there are things you can do to take control.

Shyness can feel overwhelming, and you may need on occasion to express your difficult feelings. Write yourself a letter as if you are talking to your best friend.

Dear Self,
The other day I was sitting next to my friend in the school cafeteria when Ellen, this really popular girl, and her pals sat down right next to us. (Ours was the only table that was half empty.) She kind of smiled at me and then started talking to her friends, and suddenly I couldn't talk. Sally, my friend, started to get annoyed with me, but I was afraid to open my mouth. I was afraid Ellen would hear what I said and think I was weird or stupid. So I sat there like a complete jerk stuffing my face with a tuna sandwich and not finishing this really important story I was telling Sally. I think Sally might have gotten up and left if she hadn't felt so bad for me. I am a terrible drag.

In your letter, explain how you are feeling and why. Admit to all your worst fantasies about yourself. Write down everything you wish you could say to someone else so that the other person might comfort you. Now read it over and comfort yourself. Ask yourself a helpful question as if you are the writer's friend. For instance, "When Sally got annoyed, why didn't you explain how you were feeling? She would have understood. I'll bet she's had shy feelings herself."

UNDERSTAND YOUR SHYNESS

Now that you have begun to view your shyness with a little more patience and understanding, it's time to explore the reasons for your shyness. First, you might ask yourself, "Why am I shy?" There are many possible answers to that question. Some of them may not apply to you at all, but it will be helpful to consider them anyway. Being aware of how something started is sometimes the first step toward understanding it.

You may be shy because you were born with a more retiring personality that, in combination with certain events in your life, left you with a tendency toward shyness. Most people now believe that babies are not "blank slates" when they are born; they are born with certain personality traits that may blossom forth in response to particular life experiences or circumstances.

Joe was a quiet little boy who preferred to play with his toy cars rather than with the kids who lived on his block. He might have begun to connect with other children his age as he grew older, but his family moved constantly because of his father's work. It would have been very difficult for any child in that situation to form relationships with peers, but it was especially difficult for Joe. As a result, he became more and more introverted, preferring, as he got older, to read instead of socialize. He felt very lonely, however.

Your shyness, on the other hand, may be caused by the fact that you do not have the social skills to feel comfortable with others. Some people simply do not interact naturally and easily with others. They may need to learn some basic social skills in order to feel comfortable and enjoy the positive response of others.

You may be shy because you do not feel confident about yourself. Maybe you have had one too many negative experiences with people, and this has left you feeling hurt and afraid that you simply can't measure up.

Your problem could also be rooted in the simple fact that you and others have labeled you as shy. It's a funny thing about labels. People tend to live up to them, even if they are inaccurate. If you're told you're good at something you may rise to the compliment because you feel positively motivated. But if someone hints that a specific activity is not a talent of yours, you may perform quite poorly, largely because you have lost all inspiration to do well.

As you can see, it's very easy to come by shyness. That is probably why so many people, to greater or lesser degrees, experience the condition. Now it's time to take a closer look at your particular type of shyness. Once you can identify exactly what you feel and when, you will be ready to make some changes.

WHEN ARE YOU SHY?

It is pointless to shrug your shoulders and say, "I am shy, period." Recognizing the situations that trigger your shyness is a critical part of moving past the problem. Let's take a look at a few basic questions about your particular type of shyness in order to help you isolate the areas where you need the most help.

1. In which of these situations do you feel shy?

♦ When I'm with a large group of people
♦ When I'm with a small group of people
♦ When I'm talking with one other person
♦ When I have to perform or speak in front of others
♦ When I need to ask for help
♦ When I am with someone of the opposite sex
♦ When I'm with someone new
♦ When I have to stand up for myself and be assertive
♦ All social situations in general

2. Which types of people make you feel particularly shy?

♦ Aggressive
♦ Popular
♦ Humorous
♦ Confident
♦ Shyer than I am
♦ Very attractive
♦ Sexually attractive to me
♦ Obviously interested in me as a friend
♦ Obviously interested in me romantically
♦ Authority figures
♦ People I perceive to be talented or skilled

3. When you are with these people what do you think about?

+ I worry about doing the wrong thing
+ I wonder what they expect of me
+ I wish I were somewhere else
+ I wish I were someone else
+ I am sure that I am saying or doing the wrong thing
+ I wonder if I look okay
+ I suspect that they are secretly laughing at me

4. What emotions do you experience when you feel shy?

+ Embarrassment
+ Uncertainty
+ Anger at others
+ Anger at myself
+ Frustration
+ Loneliness
+ Discomfort

5. What do you do that makes it clear to others that you are shy?

+ I speak in a low voice
+ I avoid making eye contact
+ I don't talk very much
+ I stutter a little
+ I talk on and on about nothing to fill the silence
+ I can't stop fidgeting
+ I try to escape as soon as possible
+ I avoid people as much as possible
+ I don't have a lot of friends
+ I'm often by myself

6. List the situations in which you do *not* feel shy. How do you feel at these times?

+ Relaxed
+ Welcomed
+ Confident
+ Helpful
+ Important

- ◆ Giving
- ◆ Smart
- ◆ Warm
- ◆ Accepted

Now that you have a pretty good idea of when you feel shy, in front of what people, and exactly how you feel when this shyness hits, you are ready to start changing things. As I've said before, becoming a more confident you is at the root of change.

Here are some exercises to help you gain confidence.

MOVING PAST SHYNESS
▲▼▲

The object of these exercises is twofold. One purpose is to pull you out of yourself, to force you to think about something other than where you might not measure up. The second purpose is to help you start moving past those "I wish I could disappear" feelings toward some "I've got something to offer" thoughts!

SET A REALISTIC GOAL

Considering everything you now know about your shyness, realistically set a goal for yourself. Remember what we said earlier about not trying to deny the person you truly are. Run through a scene in your mind that usually gives you a great deal of discomfort. Imagine how you feel. Now consider what small change you could make in your behavior the next time this sort of moment occurs. Then imagine some positive results. Tom, for example, cannot bear to be around big crowds. He absolutely clams up. It's impossible for him to believe that anyone cares what he has to say, given that so many other people with so much on the ball are talking. He loses interest in talking to his close buddies, too. All he can think about is how foolish and unimportant he feels and that if he opens his mouth he's bound to make a fool of himself. Tom might imagine the following scene:

He is standing with his friends outside the school when they are approached by a number of laughing and confident members of the basketball team. Cheerily they begin describing practice, and Tom feels those old terrible emotions of embarrassment and discomfort descend. But instead of clamming up, he forces himself to stop turning inward. Instead, he listens to the story and even asks a question about what one player is saying. Much to his surprise, the player responds enthusiastically, happy that someone is interested in his thoughts. He directs his remarks straight at Tom, obviously enjoying the conversation. Tom, seeing that this player is interested in his views, offers another comment, and the conversation continues. Tom no longer feels embarrassed. Instead, he feels involved.

ENCOURAGE YOURSELF

When you can see you're heading for a moment that might trigger an attack of shyness, take a deep breath and start encouraging yourself. Say things like "I can do this" and "I'm fine."

Victoria loved to play the piano, but she suffered from what her teacher called "performance anxiety." It felt like the worst kind of shyness in the world. She would take her seat at the piano, look at the audience, and want to crawl into a hole. She never seemed to play well when others were listening.

Now it was the end-of-the-year recital. The room was filled with the friendly faces of her classmates and their

parents, and still Victoria was near tears. "I can't do this," she told herself. "I never play well when..."
Victoria stopped herself. For a moment she closed her eyes and thought, "Wait a minute. Yesterday when I played this piece I was great! The neighbor across the street knocked on the door and said I sounded like a professional. I am good." Victoria felt her panic subside just a little. She was still nervous, but she was also aware of a strong possibility she'd blocked out before— she would probably play beautifully!

When negative thoughts about who you are or what you wish you had to offer threaten to move in, push them away. Work constantly on your inner feelings. Once you stop allowing negative thoughts to shake you up, your outward behavior will improve.

BE PREPARED FOR CONVERSATIONS

A common problem of shy people is that under pressure (imposed by themselves!) they have trouble coming up with things to say. Why not every week write down about five current issues that you can comfortably discuss? The topics could include social events at school, athletic competitions, upcoming tests, school vacations, or some interesting news you heard. Under each topic write down two observations that could inspire conversation. For example, if the school dance is one of your topics, you might use these observations:

♦ Last year the decorations looked kind of flimsy. Shouldn't we do something different this year?
♦ What kind of music should we have? Maybe we could get the band that played at the school in the next town. Weren't they great?

If necessary, pull these notes out several times a week and

study them. Do whatever it takes to give yourself confidence that you *will* have something to say.

STOP THINKING OF YOURSELF AS A SHY PERSON

The moment you give in to the word "shy," it will seem to have more influence over you than it actually does. Again, it's a question of labeling. Think of all the times you say to yourself, "I am so shy!" Now replace the word "shy" with another word that describes your feelings or behavior more accurately:

♦ When I was speaking to Paul I felt *insecure.*
♦ When I walked into the party late I felt *distant.*
♦ When my friend starts telling real funny jokes to a crowd I become very *quiet.*
♦ When I can't make myself heard over a bunch of kids I feel *frustrated.*

ENVISION NEW PEOPLE AS YOUR FRIENDS

In your imagination, relive a conversation you had with a friend, picturing the whole scene. Now, replace this friend with a person who makes you feel shy. But continue the conversation. Imagine being yourself with this person, without fear or embarrassment. The next time you find yourself with the person who makes you feel shy, pretend you're talking to your good friend. This will help you get used to the idea that you can be yourself in front of anyone.

REWRITE THE SHYNESS SCENE

Think of a situation in which you felt terribly shy. Now, keeping in mind your personality, imagine how that scene might have been played out had you not been feeling shy.

What would you have said? What would you have done? Don't hold back. Play the scene exactly the way you wish it had gone. Do this even if you're not really ready to have this kind of confidence yet. Imagine the positive reactions of those to whom you are talking. The next time you find yourself in a similar situation, quickly replay this rewritten scene in your mind. Then be the actor. Play the part of a confident version of yourself, even if it feels unreal. Sometimes you have to play the part first in order to actually begin to live it.

Shyness is a condition that almost all of us experience at different times in our lives. Sometimes it is a protective and positive sensation. But most times it causes a lot of distress. The worst thing you can do if you feel shy is to attack yourself because of it. Even the most timid person has moments when he or she doesn't feel shy. The best thing you can do is look for the positive side, understand your particular kind of shyness, and try to ease your way past the aspect of your shyness that causes you pain. As we've seen, the root of shyness is a lack of self-confidence. If you are shy, and if you are not feeling very good about yourself, the suggestions in this chapter can go a long way toward helping you grow and change. You don't have to be saddled with shyness that keeps you from doing what you would most like to do. But in order to move past your shyness, you do have to understand yourself, see your capacity to change, and act on that knowledge.

CONFIDENCE BUILDERS
▲▼▲

Shy people often fail to give themselves credit. They forget to concentrate on their strengths. Don't let this happen to you. Take every opportunity to remind yourself of your best attributes. Work on your strengths, and accept your weaknesses for what they are—part of human nature.

NOTE YOUR SUCCESSES

At the conclusion of each day, write down all of the occurrences that gave you a good feeling about yourself. These could include:

◆ Compliments you received
◆ Help you received
◆ An academic success
◆ A sports achievement
◆ An affectionate gesture from a friend

Next to each entry explain why it made you feel good. For instance, if you were able to comfort your friend Vivian, who was upset about her math grade, you might write, "I could tell Vivian was really listening to me. She trusts me." Or, if you win a tennis match, you might write, "Everyone congratulated me. All that practicing I put in paid off. I deserved that win." Explore each moment carefully and give yourself as much credit and respect as you deserve.

Many people with low self-esteem tend to belittle their successes. If they win a medal, they say, "Well, it was just a fluke." If they earn a high grade, they comment, "The teacher likes me." Don't fall into this trap. A success is a success. Enjoy it!

AVOID SURE FAILURES

Don't put yourself in positions that are bound to make you feel bad. If you are not a fast runner, don't try out for track. Maybe basketball is your game. If you can't sing, don't try out for the chorus. Perhaps you are more of a stage actress. Sometimes in an effort to feel good about ourselves we try in an overzealous fashion to prove we can do everything, as if admitting to a weakness here or there means we are worthless. Keep in mind that no one is good at everything. In fact, some of the people we most admire are those who have learned to capitalize on their strengths and keep their weaknesses tucked away.

Be careful, however, to recognize the difference between being afraid you won't be good at something and actually knowing a particular activity is not for you. Just because the thought of trying something gives you the jitters doesn't mean you shouldn't try it. Also, you might be very good at something but simply have performance anxiety. This is quite different from being afraid to do something because experience has taught you that you're bound to expose, unnecessarily, a weakness.

EIGHT

REJECTION: HOW TO HANDLE BEING ON THE "OUTS" WITH THE "IN" CROWD

▲▼▲

The need to belong, to be accepted, or to be approved of is a very powerful one. That's why rejection can hurt tremendously. It can feel so bad that lots of people will do almost anything to avoid the experience. They may:

♦ Do things that don't feel right
♦ Say things they don't mean
♦ Pretend to feel ways they don't actually feel
♦ Hurt their good friends
♦ Feel like phonies

None of these efforts to avoid rejection are going to feel good because they have nothing to do with the real you. They have to do with what you think others expect of you. Still, it often seems as if you have only two options: pretending to be someone you aren't, or being rejected.

But, surprise! There is a third option.

93

It's called "being different."

This isn't always easy. It takes courage and some special social skills. But it is effective. You *can* be yourself and not necessarily get rejected. Sure, there are some people who can't tolerate anyone whose views are different from their own. If your crowd reacts this way, you can bet they have plenty of problems, including a great deal of insecurity. But most people will not turn you away simply because you are an independent thinker.

HOW TO BE DIFFERENT
BUT WELL LIKED
▲▼▲

Most people will not dislike you merely because you don't think the way they do or want to spend your time exactly as they would wish you to. They *will* turn away, however, if you appear to pass judgment on their preferences. What you do should be up to you. Others deserve the same respect. If you're going to give yourself space to make your own decisions you have to allow others the same room:

- Don't put down other people's preferences. If your crowd wants to go to the pizza shop for the umpteenth time but you're sick of it, don't say, "I can't believe you guys want to go there *again!*" Instead, say something along the lines of "I'm just not in the mood. I'm tired of pizza. Could we try someplace else this time?" This kind of comment will serve you much better.
- Don't lecture people. If your crowd wants to do something you think is wrong, like crash a party or drink beer, don't tell them what's right or wrong as if you're a parent or a teacher. Express your thoughts in terms of how you feel. "I don't feel comfortable about crashing Sue's party. I wasn't invited. If you guys decide to do that I'll just go home."

♦ Remember you're allowed to have your own interests. If everyone wants to go to the baseball game but you'd rather play tennis, don't agree to go just because you want to be included. You might be excluded if you said, "I can't believe you guys like baseball. I hate it!" Instead, simply say, "Have a good time. It's a big game today. But you know, I'd rather play tennis." This will show your respect for the way your friends feel and open the door for them to tolerate your preferences.

♦ Invite people to join you. Sometimes when you want to do something different from the crowd, you may worry that you'll be rejected. Instead of fretting, you could invite the whole crowd to come with you to another activity. "I don't want to spend the afternoon in the park. I'd rather go to the folk concert at the mall. Why don't you come, too?"

♦ Keep in touch. Even if your own interests have kept you too busy all week to spend a single afternoon with the crowd, make an effort to stay in touch. Call a few friends. Tell them what you've been doing and ask how they are. Make it clear that even though you're busy, you still care.

When going your own way it's very important to show respect for all the other ways people choose to go. If you do this and are still rejected, you can bet the rejection has little to do with you. Only those who are very insecure and filled with doubts about themselves would turn away from someone else simply because he or she has chosen to be different.

HOW TO HANDLE REJECTION
▲▼▲

Rejection is difficult to handle. It can stir up all the doubts you have ever had about yourself. It can make you feel unattractive, unimportant, and unwanted.

But worst of all, it can make you feel unattached... as if you haven't a good friend in the world.

Of course, more than likely, this will not happen. But it is a good place to begin when considering how to cope with the pain of rejection. If it seems you are being left out of the crowd, here are ten steps you can take:

1. Allow yourself to feel the pain. There's no point in hiding from it. It's important to take the time to "lick your wounds" and let the difficult feelings subside. Sometimes it seems easier to hide from painful thoughts. But you can never really run from hurt. It's always there somewhere. If you don't face it honestly, it will simply sit in your unconscious—the part of your mind where thoughts exist that you are not aware of. Far from remaining silent, however, at various times these thoughts may cause you to behave in ways that are destructive to you and to others.

Lacey could not believe that everyone had turned on her so quickly. Peggy and Jean had seemed to be such good friends. How could they have believed the terrible rumor that Lacey had tried to steal Peggy's boyfriend? They hadn't even wanted to hear her side of the story. It seemed, in fact, that only Lacey's old friend Priscilla believed her. "I don't care about them anyway," Lacey said to herself over and over as she prepared to attend the Saturday night dance.

Much to her relief she spotted Priscilla the moment she walked in and made a beeline for her side. Seeing a number of kids whispering about her, Lacey began to laugh very loud as she chatted away with Priscilla and another girl, who was not a member of the crowd Lacey had traveled with. "I feel great," Lacey assured herself as she looked around the room at all of her ex-friends. "Who cares about them?"

Suddenly Priscilla said, "Excuse me for a min-

ute. I'm going to talk with Rob."
*"Wait," Lacey practically cried out, as much to
her surprise as Priscilla's.*
*"What am I supposed to do?" Priscilla shrugged.
"I'll be back. Promise."*
*But Lacey couldn't stop herself. "Some friend
you are," she spat. Instantly she was sickened by her
own behavior. But what made her feel even worse
was the angry look that had settled on Priscilla's
face.*

Lacey, deep inside, was still hurting, and as soon as
Priscilla did something that inadvertently forced her
to face that pain, she struck out—unfortunately, at the
wrong person.

2. Consider who is doing the rejecting. Sometimes we get
   so caught up with being "dumped" that we fail to
   remember that part of the rejection may have been our
   choice. If you did something you felt was right but your
   crowd turned on you because of it, then they are not
   the only ones doing the rejecting. In deciding to follow
   your own beliefs, you rejected their views. This
   thought can be very comforting and can offer you a
   measure of strength when you're coping with being
   left behind. After all, it's not just rejection you feel.
   You might also be disappointed and angry with your
   friends. It's all too easy to forget this fact when the
   pain of rejection hits.

3. Don't leap into another crowd or instantly form a fresh
   circle of "best friends." Jumping into a whole new
   group without recovering from your hurt is a form of
   running away. When you run away, you are thinking
   more about what you've left behind than about where
   you're going. And as a result, the place where you end
   up may not be the right place for you. After a short
   while you may discover these new "friends" have very

little in common with you, and then you will feel lonelier than ever. Not to mention the fact that ultimately you will walk away from them, or they from you, and the cycle of rejection will continue.

4. Remind yourself of your strengths. Refer back to the work you did earlier in this book. What is unique about you? Create a new list, entitled "What I Can Offer in a Friendship." List all of your good traits that friends have enjoyed.

5. Become involved with new people. This might mean joining a club or a team or attending a school event you might otherwise have skipped. Getting involved with a group of people who have a common interest or cause will immediately give you a base on which to build friendships. At first the things you do together will be related to the activity, but if you find someone with whom you are compatible the relationship will certainly grow. Joining a team or club or regularly attending certain events will give you an opportunity to feel connected with other people.

6. Don't bad-mouth anyone. You may be tempted, as you find yourself making new friends, to put down the people who turned their backs on you. Don't do it! First of all, it will give the impression that you talk behind people's backs. That could make your new friends feel very uncertain about how much they can trust you. Second, bad-mouthing your former pals is a sign of your own insecurity. Your time is better spent moving forward in a positive way. Besides, at some point you might want to renew your friendship with those people. Keeping your mouth closed about them will safeguard that opportunity.

7. Try to remember that in terms of friendships, all crowds are equal. The popular crowd offers no more in terms of loyalty, warmth, comfort, generosity, or un-

derstanding than any other. They may simply offer more glitz. If the popular crowd has bid you a not very fond farewell, try not to feel that the next crowd you get into is second best. After all, second best to what? Obviously the popular crowd wasn't best for you. If they had been, they might have treated you better. Look at this new crowd in terms of what the individual members and you have to offer one another instead of in terms of where they, and therefore you, rank on some social scale.

Lana was finally making friends again. It had been weeks since Tina and her collection of friends had dumped her, and at last Lana was getting busy again. The trouble was, she couldn't help feeling as if she'd gone down a notch. Before, with Tina, she'd been with people she thought were really special, but now she was with a bunch of nice, but ordinary, friends. She found herself looking over her shoulder a lot at Tina's crowd in the lunchroom, wondering what they were doing or thinking.

One weekend she grudgingly agreed to go with her new friends to the ice-skating rink. She was a terrible skater, and when she got on the ice she panicked. "What if everyone's better than me?" she thought to herself. She could see Tina across the rink making fun of her. She looked around. The truth was, everyone was better than she was. But the next thing she knew, two new friends took her arms and guided her encouragingly around the ice. Lana looked at them with surprise and pleasure, and for the first time she began to feel lucky.

8. If you feel as if your friends are giving you the cold shoulder, remind yourself that it can't last. Sometimes, within a large group, a kind of subgroup will develop. This subgroup may gang up on one member. Deep down, these people are probably more motivated

by their own need to feel superior than by anything that person has done. But if this happens to you, don't despair. The members of this united front will soon get bored. Just give them time. Try to concentrate on some hobbies, spend a bit more time with your family, and whatever you do, don't hide! If you don't act guilty or scared, the snub will disappear that much faster.

9. Since rejection is something everyone experiences sooner or later in life, why not open up the subject to real friends and family? Talk about it! Listen to what they reveal about their experiences with rejection. You might be surprised to hear how keenly they felt all the things you are now feeling! And you may be inspired by the ways in which all of them managed to survive the pain and go on to much happier times.

10. Remind yourself that rejection is an experience, not a disaster. Disasters are events that have a negative impact on people for a long time, often for the rest of their lives. Rejections feel embarrassing and painful when they are happening. But then they are over. Try to remember that once you recover from a rejection, nothing else about your life need be colored by the experience, except in the most positive way. Rejection usually makes us a little stronger and a little wiser. Who wouldn't want that?

HOW TO LOSE YOUR POPULARITY GRACEFULLY
—————————— ▲▼▲ ——————————

When you're up on a pedestal it can feel, as we said before, both terrific and scary. It's wonderful to be admired, but it's frightening to realize it could all go away tomorrow.

So let's imagine it *is* tomorrow. Just last month you were

riding high, and now the tide has turned and you are no longer the admired one. It's not that you've done anything cruel or selfish. It's simply that everyone's attention has shifted. You feel hurt and embarrassed. You feel like a has-been.

Is it time to crawl into a hole? Absolutely not. It's time, in fact, to truly step forward. In a way, you're now free to be who you really are. So...

1. Don't struggle to win people back. You can't. Again, popularity is not something you can control. You might attract a few people back by doing them favors or trying to please them, but in the end you will lose them, too. That's not friendship. That's bribery. And bribery will never bring popularity.

2. Work on strengthening the true friendships you still have. Don't make your real friends feel as if being the big cheese is more important to you than they are. Don't spend your time howling about how hurt you feel because you have lost so many pals. It will make your true buddies feel as if they don't count. Let them know how much you appreciate the friendship and support they have always offered you. Words aren't necessary. Being there with warmth and sincere interest is enough.

3. Don't torture yourself by thinking about what you could have done differently. You have no way of knowing how things might have turned out if you had taken another road. Besides, chances are you were just doing your own thing when suddenly the attention of the crowd shifted. Remember, popularity is not within your control. What you do does not necessarily determine the crowd's opinion.

4. Have faith in yourself. Perhaps you have been yourself all along, but a lot of other kids have decided you're no longer interesting. That doesn't mean you are not good

enough. It simply means the crowd is ready for something new. That's fine, but you are not a circus act. You are a person. Real friends want you to be consistent. Then again, maybe you've been putting on a show all along, and now the crowd has decided to buy tickets to something else. Now's the time to think about letting the real you step forward. After all, you have nothing to lose! And you might be surprised to discover the real you has a lot more staying power.

5. Give yourself some time to put the issue of popularity in its place. You've learned that popularity is not the answer to life's woes. In fact, it can create problems of its own. Give yourself a chance to feel good about an entirely different set of circumstances such as having a few close buddies with whom you can really be yourself. Now you can do just what you'd like without fear of losing the admiring glances of others. And since fewer people are watching, you can enjoy the freedom to try new things and fall flat on your face! It won't matter. Because your real friends will be right there to help you up.

BEING AN INDEPENDENT OPERATOR
▲▼▲

Belonging to a particular crowd or group is not for everyone. Some people enjoy the friendship of lots of different kids from many different circles. They choose their friends strictly on the basis of shared experiences and interests. It doesn't matter at all which crowd these friends are a part of.

This takes a lot of confidence and a strong sense of self. People who are happy not belonging to any one crowd feel easy about not labeling themselves in any particular way. They feel comfortable with all of the different sides of their own personalities. These people are not nearly as concerned with having a set group of kids to count on as they are with finding companionship for all the many different activities they enjoy and the varied feelings they need to share.

Jason was a terrific athlete. He also liked to write poetry. He enjoyed using words and a basketball to express himself. He felt there was something beautifully rhythmic about both. Unfortunately, his teammates teased him a lot about the pad and pen he carried with him everywhere so that he could write down phrases and thoughts that came to him. But the teasing didn't bother James that much. For one thing, he knew his teammates kind of admired his writing, and for another, he'd started a poetry club at school and had plenty of people with whom he could discuss his thoughts. Those people teased him about being a jock. But James just laughed. He thought it was terrific to have such different but fulfilling interests.

Lots of kids fear that if they don't belong to any one crowd, popular or not, they will be left out. This is not so. Yes, they may upset some of the members of a crowd with whom they spend a lot of time. They may be accused of being disloyal or not knowing who their real friends are. But the truth is, people in a crowd like one another, but they get tired of always looking at the same faces. It's lovely to have friends outside the pack. And independent people get a major bonus. Often they receive more invitations than anyone to go out and do things. Since they don't belong to any one group, they are perceived as being available to everyone.

There's no doubt about it. Being rejected—whether you are kicked out of a crowd, lose your popular status, or simply opt to be yourself and then find yourself with fewer friends—can be upsetting.

Being rejected challenges your sense of self. It brings into question and consideration all those things about yourself that you find troubling or unsatisfactory. And it tests your ability to accept who you are and your ability to grow and change.

In order to cope with rejection throughout your life—and it will come up in different forms—you do need to have a confident center. You need to believe in what is good about you and your ability to keep growing and improving. Because in the end being popular with yourself is the only popularity contest you should ever want to be in!

CONFIDENCE BUILDERS

When rejection hits, most people's first reaction is something like "What's wrong with me!" or "I wasn't good enough!" Everything revolves around their feelings of inadequacy. They forget to consider that more than one person is involved in a rejection. There is at least one other person in this painful experience, and he or she is very human. What does that mean? The rejection you have experienced is not just about you and your problems. It's about this other person's problems as well.

UNDERSTAND THAT A REJECTION IS NOT JUST ABOUT YOU

Remind yourself that there are two sides to every story and that most people have lots of secrets and fears you don't know about. If you are rejected by someone, consider the possibility that it had nothing to do with you. This person may be angry, sad, or afraid of things you don't know about. Don't assume a rejection is all about what's wrong with you. It's also about what goes on inside the other person. She may have:

• Just had a fight with another friend

- Failed a test that you aced
- Seen her parents have another major argument
- Woken up, looked in the mirror, and felt ugly
- Taken one look at you and felt terribly jealous

Ironically, sometimes when we are rejected it's because people think the world of us. They can't tolerate their own feelings of inadequacy, and so they get rid of us before we can get rid of them! The next time someone turns you away, instead of instantly thinking, "What did I do wrong?" why not think, "I wonder what's going on with him?"

You can bet there's a lot.

NINE

KIDS TALK
ABOUT
POPULARITY

▲▼▲

I t is all too easy to think that we are alone in the difficult and confusing feelings we experience in day-to-day life. Everyone else may seem to feel just fine. You may think that all those glittering people around you have no terrible moments of self-doubt or envy or resentment. Conversely, you might believe that all of the quiet and shy people you know are unhappy, that they would like nothing more than to be a part of the "in" crowd.

The truth is, everyone sees things through the prism of their own problems. This means that the way we interpret a situation has more to do with our feelings than with the facts. If we're afraid of feeling all alone, then we may think that a shy person is miserable. If we think popularity would solve all of our problems, then we may assume that popular people don't have a care in the world.

In reality people are far too complicated to be pegged quite so easily. The more realistically we look at those people who affect our lives, the better able we will be to understand them and to give ourselves a break.

So the next time you find yourself feeling all alone, hurt, rejected, or sure that everyone thinks you're worthless and unimportant, consider what the following people have to say about how they feel. Things are never the way they seem.

AMY

AGE THIRTEEN

▲▼▲

I'm pretty popular. The phone rings a lot for me, and I always do things with friends, like going out for pizza or sitting in the park. I think I'm nice-looking, too. But there is this one girl in class who makes me feel awful. You wouldn't know it. I mean I don't ever talk to her, and I'm not even sure she knows my last name! Still, when I see her with her friends, I feel so envious. I can't figure out why. I just get this feeling that what she's got is better than what I've got. I don't ever tell my friends how I feel. I don't want to hurt them. Besides, I wouldn't know what to say. I don't understand myself sometimes.

DAVID

AGE FOURTEEN

▲▼▲

I hang out with some guys in school, and I guess you could say they're popular. They're real good at sports, and the girls seem to like them a lot. These guys include me in everything they do, but they also kind of laugh at me. I'm not that great an athlete, and the girls up until now have not been that interested in me. But just last week this one real pretty girl named Liza started paying attention to me. Well, the guys can't believe it. They don't stop teasing me. I laugh, as if I think it's funny, but really I feel insulted. Why shouldn't Liza like me? Just because I'm not captain of the basketball team?

MOLLY

AGE THIRTEEN
▲▼▲

Last year I was the new girl in school. I still had a little baby fat left, and I think I looked kind of immature. Most of the really cool kids totally ignored me. Except for one. Her name was Julie. She was the hippest one of all. It was clear she didn't care what anyone thought. Julie had a great figure, beautiful blond hair, and a very wicked sense of humor. It was funny, but it could border on being mean. Anyway, she decided I was okay. She made dates with me, and we hung out together sometimes in the park or painting—we both liked to paint a lot. Anyway, I couldn't believe it. I kept waiting for her friends to ditch her, but they never did. I guess she was just too strong. Actually, what happened was that they started to be nicer to me. Now it's a year later, and I look more mature. All of us are friends now. I will always remember Julie for the way she befriended me, and I'm going to try to do the same for someone else.

AMANDA

AGE TWELVE
▲▼▲

I don't have a lot of friends. I have Terry and Marie most of all, and I sometimes hang out with a few others. The truth is, I love music and art and spend a lot of time by myself doing those things. Usually I feel fine about that. But sometimes, like when there's a school dance, I feel a little out of it. I look around the room and wish I could think of things to say to all those people. But then I start chatting with my good friends, and I feel better. And when a few people I don't know very well join us, I feel fine. Sometimes I talk a lot and sometimes I don't. But whatever I do, it almost always feels okay.

MATTHEW

AGE FOURTEEN
▲▼▲

I'm short. It makes me angry that the real popular guys at school are tall. So I've been doing some weight lifting. I use my older brother's equipment. I also pretend that I'm not upset. I act as if I don't care whether people like me or not. I spend a lot of time fantasizing about how in the end I'll get the prettiest girl, get into the best college, and make the most money. But in the meantime I just pretend that nothing bothers me. My best friend knows how I feel, but we don't talk much about it.

ROSA

AGE FIFTEEN
▲▼▲

Everyone seems to think I'm beautiful, except me. I always have dates, but truthfully I don't know if any of those boys really like me or not. I went out with one guy, and I later discovered he asked me out on a dare. Some other guy had bet him that I'd say no. My life probably sounds like fun and . . . well, sometimes it is. But other times, when I'm alone, I get to feeling a little hollow. Sure, I'd rather be pretty than not. I like having a good figure, and I think I'm quite smart. But sometimes I think people figure my life is perfect. It isn't. My parents argue a lot at home, and that makes me unhappy. And I don't think I have such a great personality. Lots of times I run out of things to say. And I can't tell funny stories nearly as well as my friend. It's embarrassing.

NEAL

AGE FIFTEEN
▲▼▲

Popularity means close to nothing to me. In fact, I think it's a silly word. I have my friends. Sometimes I find myself alone, but I don't feel lonely when that happens. I read or watch TV or lie on my bed and try to dream up some incredible machine I'm going to invent. Sure, sometimes I get down on myself, but who doesn't? Like the time I had a thing for this girl Vivienne and she wasn't interested. That didn't feel good. But I got over it. You can't win 'em all.

JOANNA

AGE TWELVE
▲▼▲

I don't know what happened. For a few months everyone wanted to be with me. But then suddenly Linda took over. I would have felt totally awful if it hadn't been for my friend Beth. She told me she'd like me no matter what. That helped. I mean, I didn't like going into school for a while because I felt so weird and let down. I was sure people were laughing at me, which I now realize wasn't so. But then I noticed Linda wasn't the center of attention either after a while. That's when I really started to feel better. I guess this stuff happens to everyone.

JOAN

AGE FOURTEEN
▲▼▲

I want to be popular. It's fun. I flirt with lots of guys and choose my clothes really carefully so I look sexy. People who say they don't care about being popular are lying. Sure it's scary sometimes. I don't always feel like myself. And the other day my friend Sarah said she overheard someone say I'm not "real." That made me feel bad. But that person's probably not "real" either. I was fat and ugly for years, and suddenly this year I got cute, so I'm taking advantage of it. If I could be popular just being myself I would. But who wants to hang out with someone who wears unimportant clothes and who doesn't let boys get anywhere near her? No one. That's who.

Popularity is not what it seems. Neither are people. When it comes to leading a happy life, it's not who admires or approves of us that counts. It's how we feel about ourselves that really matters. It's not the number of people who surround us every day that means something, but rather the quality of the friendships that we enjoy.

When people are popular they receive a great deal of flattery and attention. That can feel great. And from the outside it certainly looks like fun. But attention doesn't always feel real, warm, comforting, and understanding.

So if you're popular, enjoy it—but don't depend on it and don't neglect your friendships. And if you aren't popular but wish you were, don't keep trying to make it happen. Nothing will erode your confidence more quickly than trying to accomplish something over which you have little to no control. Instead, take the time to appreciate who you are. If you like yourself, other people will, too. And if popularity does result, it will be the kind that can't let you down...because no matter what happens you'll always have your very best friend. You!

BIBLIOGRAPHY

Carnegie, Dale. *How to Win Friends and Influence People.* New York: Pocket Books, Simon & Schuster, 1982.

Gabor, Don. *How to Talk to the People You Love.* New York: Fireside, Simon & Schuster, 1989.

Schneider, Meg. *Help! I Can't Think of a Thing to Say.* Middletown, Conn.: Field Publications, 1987.

Schneider, Meg. *Love Cycles: The Many Faces of Romance.* New York: Berkley Books, 1985.

Zimbardo, Philip G. *Shyness.* Reading, Mass.: Addison-Wesley Publishing, 1977.

INDEX

ABOUT THE AUTHOR

Meg F. Schneider grew up in New York City and now lives in Westchester County with her husband and two small sons. She remembers being concerned with issues of popularity while growing up and wishes she'd understood then what really mattered.

Ms. Schneider has a master's degree in counseling from Columbia University and has written many self-help books for young people on amongst other subjects, difficult romantic situations, conversation techniques, and social savvy. She is currently writing a fiction series which deals with many of the issues found in POPULARITY HAS ITS UPS AND DOWNS.

DATE DUE			

12014

158
SCH

Schneider, Meg F.

Popularity has its
ups and downs.